9/11 C05 07 2. IC

C05 07 8 1
14 IC1

D0408969

RL

Ambrose Bierce
and the
Ace of Shoots

AMBROSE BIERCE

and the

ACE OF SHOOTS

Oakley Hall

VIKING

VIKING
Published by the Penguin Group
Penguin Group (USA) Inc., 375 Hudson Street, New York, New York 10014, U.S.A.
Penguin Group (Canada), 10 Alcorn Avenue, Toronto, Ontario, Canada M4V 3B2
 (a division of Pearson Penguin Canada Inc.)
Penguin Books Ltd, 80 Strand, London WC2R 0RL, England
Penguin Ireland, 25 St. Stephen's Green, Dublin 2, Ireland
 (a division of Penguin Books Ltd)
Penguin Books Australia Ltd, 250 Camberwell Road, Camberwell, Victoria 3124, Australia
 (a division of Pearson Australia Group Pty Ltd)
Penguin Books India Pvt Ltd, 11 Community Centre, Panchsheel Park,
 New Delhi - 110 017, India
Penguin Group (NZ), Cnr Airborne and Rosedale Roads,
 Albany, Auckland 1310, New Zealand (a division of Pearson New Zealand Ltd)
Penguin Books (South Africa) (Pty) Ltd, 24 Sturdee Avenue,
 Rosebank, Johannesburg 2196, South Africa

Penguin Books Ltd, Registered Offices: 80 Strand, London WC2R 0RL, England

First published in 2005 by Viking Penguin, a member of Penguin Group (USA) Inc.

10 9 8 7 6 5 4 3 2 1

PUBLISHER'S NOTE
This is a work of fiction. Names, characters, places, and incidents either are the product of the
author's imagination or are used fictitiously, and any resemblance to actual persons, living or
dead, business establishments, events, or locales is entirely coincidental.

LIBRARY OF CONGRESS CATALOGING IN PUBLICATION DATA
Hall, Oakley M.
 Ambrose Bierce and the ace of shoots / Oakley Hall.
 p.   cm.
 ISBN 0-670-03390-1
 1. Bierce, Ambrose, 1842–1914?—Fiction.   2. Fugitives from justice—Fiction.
3. Shooters of firearms—Fiction.   4. Journalists—Fiction.   5. California—Fiction.   I. Title.
PS3558.A373A796 2005
813'.54—dc22   2004057181

This book is printed on acid-free paper.

Printed in the United States of America
Set in Granjon with Bandicoot Display
Designed by Elke Sigal

CHAPTER ONE

EXILE, n. *One who serves his country by residing abroad, yet is not an ambassador.*

— *The Devil's Dictionary*

SUNDAY, MARCH 6, 1892

Just before the Colonel Studely Wild West Show tragedies, because of an attack of asthma and the importunities of a young poetess, Ambrose Bierce had exiled himself to the Putnam House hotel in Auburn, in the foothills of the Sierra Nevada.

Auburn was a stop on my journey to an interview arranged by Sam Chamberlain, managing editor of the San Francisco *Examiner,* and I had just enough time to pay a quick visit to Bierce.

He was taking the air on the veranda of the hotel, on a hill overlooking the town, dressed in his customary black suiting and high collar, his hat tilted on his forehead against the mountain sun—Bitter Bierce, Almighty God Bierce, the critical and ethical Grand Cham of San Francisco. For a month he had been sending his Sunday column, "Prattle," down to the *Examiner* by train.

I was afraid he would think I had traveled all this distance just to call on him, and, in the confusion of his emotions, become excessively standoffish and sarcastic. But he put aside the newspaper he had been reading and leaped from his chair, calling out, "Tom Redmond!"

We shook hands heartily. I asked if he was enjoying his Auburn rustication.

He bared his teeth beneath his mustache. "We are told, Friend Tom, that hell is a place of endless torture by fire. I believe it is a place of endless boredom."

I said I was not sure that the San Francisco offices of the *Examiner* could be considered heaven.

"By comparison merely. And what are you doing up here, Tom?"

"I'm to interview Oz Bird."

"The train robber!"

"He's up in these foothills somewhere. He wants to tell his story to the *Examiner*."

"That name brings to mind the old Hungry Valley shootings," Bierce said. "How is the interview to be effected, Tom?"

"I'm to hire a horse at Jenning's Livery Stables and set out on the road to Colfax. I'll be contacted along the way, after they have ascertained that I am not accompanied by a posse."

"Many deserted mining camps in these hills," Bierce said.

Indeed, I had given some thought to being tossed down an old mine shaft by a murderous train robber and his gang.

Frowning, Bierce asked, "Wasn't there a wife who was an exhibition shooter as well?"

"Dora Pratt. She's with Colonel Studely's Wild West Show, which is in fact coming to San Francisco next week."

"Be careful, Tom!"

I missed working with Bierce on murder cases in the City, and here I was on my own, advised to be careful.

"Has the foothill air had the desired effect?" I asked.

He nodded, but with a light snoring sound. Bierce usually departed from the city when he had had an attack of asthma, but there had been an additional reason for this adjournment.

"What of the fair-haired poet from Sausalito?" I asked.

He sighed. "What could I have been thinking? The demands of a woman who has surrendered some insignificant aspect of herself to a man can be flabbergasting."

Changing the subject, he told me he had been reading Sunday's *Examiner,* and he pointed to the women's column, on the same page as "Prattle." Its author, Miss Keith, had only recently been hired by Willie Hearst.

"For instance," Bierce said. "You are aware of my attitude toward female journalists. I disapprove of the Daughters of Thunder moving in to male employments, with their desire to achieve familiarity without contempt. Miss Keith makes the usual henarchist complaints, but it is difficult for me to dispute a female who shares my own attitudes toward religious bosh."

He had gone on record describing the contents of women's cranimums as "brainettes made of gray batter."

"Have you met her?" he asked.

I had not.

"I imagine her as a prim member of her gender, with nose-pincher eyeglasses and lips as thin as razors," Bierce said, and walked with me to the railing, where we gazed out over the town of Auburn, stretched out below.

....

"You have a dangerous mission, Tom," he said as we shook hands good-bye. "Should you take along my revolver?"

I said I thought I would be safer without it, as I would be better able to carry Oz Bird's side of the story to the *Examiner* alive than dead. I then headed for Jenning's Livery Stable, and my interview with the train robber.

....

I didn't know how long it took us; the two men who met me on the trail blindfolded me and escorted me into the hills. My horse was led upgrade and steeply down, and steeply up again—a passage of three canyons, with a bottle of water sometimes passed to me, and once some bread and hard cheese.

Then I was dismounted, shoved up two steps, and seated in a hard chair with my blindfold still in place. Three voices conversed, two of them familiar to me as the men who had escorted me here, and a third, deep, harsh, and dominating.

When the bandanna was finally removed from my eyes, there was only one man in the room, seating himself after stripping off my blindfold. Oswald Bird faced me across a pine tabletop, a lean-faced man with a short crop of beard. Pale eyes regarded me out of a prison pallor. We were in a log-walled room, chinked with mud, and with a window on blue sky and the tops of pines.

"You are Mr. Hearst's fellow?" His was the harsh voice.

"My name is Redmond."

I could see the butt of the bowie knife that was holstered on his belt. He wore a blue work shirt, open at the throat, where the skin had the same pallor as his face. At the corner of one of his eyes was a pucker of flesh, some kind of scar. His lips were flat and severe in the mask of his whiskers. He tensed slightly as I reached for my notebook.

"You have information for the *Examiner,* Mr. Bird?"

"I do."

"You completed your prison term last month, and ten days ago you and an accomplice stopped a train down at Clary Junction, shot a guard, and rode away with thirty thousand dollars."

"Eighteen thousand!" he said, baring his teeth.

It was entirely possible that the SP Railroad had lied about the number of greenbacks aboard the train.

"When you get out of the hoosegow, you need some money to make a start," he said in a reasonable tone.

"Norman Weems was the guard's name," I said. He had been all but cut in half by the shotgun blast.

"Still be kicking if he'd done what he was told," Bird said.

"Your accomplice shot him?" I asked.

After a pause, Bird said, "*I* shot him."

"You robbed the SP because you have a grudge against the Railroad?"

He swiped the back of his hand across his lips and nodded. "Grudge is correct, mister. I would like to cut the nuts off everyone from Mr. Collis Huntington right down the line to Arliff K. Potter."

"Who is Arliff K. Potter?"

"That's the yellow-bellied sapsucker that got me into the Brewer Farm business. That is not a bald noodle I will forget soon. Nor him me, I can promise you!

"Eight years outten my life!" he said, wiping his lips on his shirt cuff.

Like Norman Weems, four Hungry Valley farmers had lost the whole rest of their lives.

"Went down there perfectly legal, and deputized to take over the Brewer Farm, make a new life for me and my wife," he said. "First thing I know, about a dozen of them sandlappers threw down on us!"

"Four of them were killed," I said.

"What'd they expect?"

"They thought they were protecting their farms."

"Wasn't their farms anymore," Bird said. "The Brewer place had been properly foreclosed on. Well, I never did blame those fellows much, except they was too fast on the trigger. The Railroad promised them the land at a certain price—I forget what it was—and then when they made that place blossom, reneged on them."

"You were selected because you were a known sharpshooter, and the Railroad thought the farmers would be cowed by that?"

"Cowed was what they wasn't!" Bird said. "They had a regular army of them, with a fellow yelling out commands. Everything but a bugle! 'Buzzard' and 'Gizzard' they called us."

"You and Guttman hid out in a cornfield until you surrendered to the sheriff the next morning. What happened to Guttman?"

Bird shrugged elaborately. "Got away down the river. Or didn't."

He described the famous shoot-out in some detail, although he did not recall the names of the men he had killed. He called them "the one with the overalls," "the one on the white horse," "the one that was yelling out orders," and so forth.

He told his story with some impatience that I did not write fast enough.

" 'Make a new life for you and your wife,' " I quoted back to him. "Why was that?"

He scowled at me. "Dora and me was sick to death of Wild West shooting stunts, and Robbie Studely in particular, and this was a fine farm raising corn and beans and vegetables, and an orchard on the way, and a six-room house, I was told. A better life! That is a powerful thing.

"The SP gimme a lawyer, name of Dinwiddy, to defend me. Turned right over on his back and give it up, like his bosses told him to. The SP was getting blamed plenty in the newspapers for the shoot-up, and they decided to nail it on Oz Bird!"

"Dinwiddy," I said, jotting down the name.

"Have to dig him up to shoot him," Bird said. "Dead as mutton. I hope he died hard!"

He railed on, detailing indignities, wrongs, and betrayals; the sneaking, scabby, perfidious, lying, pettifogging, contemptible scoundrels who operated the Southern Pacific Railroad—mainly, one Arliff K. Potter.

"Mrs. Bird divorced you when you were in prison?"

"Yep."

"Was that because of the shooting, and your conviction?"

"I don't know what it was because of. She never answered one letter of mine I wrote her! But I do know it was Robbie Studely's doing. That scurvy sneaking toad has got plenty coming to him. Count on that!"

I had not seen Colonel Studely's Show when it had come to Sacramento when I was a boy, nor in San Francisco some years later. The former Mrs. Bird, Dora Pratt, was featured now.

"Miss Pratt is one of the world's best wingshots, I understand," I said.

Bird's teeth showed among his whiskering. "Owes it all to me! Taught her everything she knows. *Showed* her. Made her!"

He chewed on his wife's disloyalty and ingratitude. "Never trust anything don't have a dick on it, that's my advice!" he said.

He began talking about his childhood. "Brought up right near here, in Placer County," he said. "Grew up shooting. Everybody I knew was handy with a rifle and sidearm. I was the handiest. Worked for Texas Jack. First time I saw that little girl I was a goner.

"Studely's doing," he said again. "We'd been working for him for two years. When I was in Quentin, he made over her, eddicated her, took her to Europe and showed her off to dukes and such over there. The Queen! It was Robbie Studely turned her against me!"

I had thought his eyes the coldest I had ever looked into, but now he blinked and looked away from me, and down.

"She'll come along when I come after her," he reassured himself. "She'll come along when I head for points south. Snap my fingers, she'll come along. Promise you that."

"So," I said, "you have some accounts to pay. The SP."

He nodded—too long a nod, it seemed to me.

"Arliff K. Potter."

He showed me his teeth again, nodding.

"Colonel Studely?"

Another nod.

"And your wife will come back to you?"

"She's my wife, whatever some divorce paper says."

"Tell me, Mr. Bird," I said, my eyes fixed on his shirt pocket. "When I write this story, am I to warn these people of your . . . intentions?"

"Warn 'em," he said, nodding. "Warn the pissant root-hog bastards! Warn 'em," he said again. "Let 'em sweat. That *is* what you are here for, innit?"

I put together a shrug and a nod that seemed to satisfy him.

"There is going to be a reckoning with Oz Bird," he said in his harsh voice. "Tell 'em that!"

We sat in silence for a while, then he hiked himself up and jammed the bandanna down on my head, pulling hair as he did so, and yelled in his hard voice, "Jukes!"

CHAPTER TWO

REPARATION, n. *Satisfaction that is made for a wrong and deducted from the satisfaction felt in committing it.*
— *The Devils's Dictionary*

TUESDAY, MARCH 8, 1892

Young William Randolph Hearst's dictum was that the reader should exclaim "Gee whiz!" upon reading the news on the first page of the *Examiner,* "Holy Moses!" at the second page, and "God Almighty!" at the third. My interview with Oswald Bird was "Gee whiz" material. Sam Chamberlain and I rewrote my story together:

BIRD VOWS VENGEANCE

EXCLUSIVE INTERVIEW WITH THE TRAIN ROBBER

OSWALD BIRD'S BETRAYERS WARNED

I was called into Willie Hearst's office and commended. He came around the desk to shake my hand in his queer, formal way. I was "Mr. Redmond" to him, for he called all his employees by their patronmics. He had, however, a handclasp like a peeled banana.

"Very well done, Mr. Redmond! The *Examiner* is proud of that story. I wonder if there might be more interviews with Mr. Bird."

I expressed interest.

"It is quite a coincidence that Colonel Studely's Wild West Show is on its way to town," I said, "considering Bird's comments on the colonel and his former wife."

"Not at all, Mr. Redmond," Willie said. "I believe the coming of the Show to the City was the reason Mr. Bird made contact with me instead of a Sacramento newspaper. There is interest in the old Hungry Valley shoot-out; will you investigate?"

"Should I go down there?"

"I think that is called for."

....

There followed meetings with the San Francisco chief of detectives, Dan O'Brien, and the railroad chief detective, a man named Culver who stored a tobacco chaw in his cheek and regularly bent forward to ring the spittoon. I learned that all law officers in California were on the lookout for Oz Bird, who was regarded as a mad-dog killer.

Last of all, I contacted Sheriff Bill Williamson of Tulare County from the telephone in Willie's office and arranged to meet him and some of the settlers who had been witness to the Hungry Valley shoot-out.

In the morning I was southbound.

WEDNESDAY, MARCH 9, 1892

On the train, chuffing through the flat, brown lowlands of the great valley of central California, bordered by the invisible coast range to the west and the misty, snow-capped Sierra to the east, I watched the dry landscape of California unroll outside my window. Sometimes I caught sight of the locomotive in its gleaming potency, leading the way on a long arc.

I worried about my mother's demand that I marry a nice Catholic girl and give her a grandchild, and I worried about my own life slowly unrolling like the landscape outside the window of the train.

....

Sheriff Williamson was a white-haired, red-faced man who occupied so much of the seat of the buggy that there was hardly room for me. He sat nodding and glowering and saying nothing while I brought him up to date on my session with Oz Bird.

The sheriff would escort me to the valley, where I would put up for the night with a farmer named Burchard, who was the settlers' authority on the shoot-out.

The valley was hardly a valley at all, bordered by low hills that were hardly hills—Bosque Valle, or Hungry Valley, so-called from the early years when settlers on the railroad lands had gone hungry bringing their acres to fruition.

"Miserable business," the sheriff said, giving his mare a whip snap to get her started. "Like all things like that, it dint have to happen, except for a couple of hardheads that made it have to happen—Henry McDermot that organized the farmers to arm themselves, and that SP fellow that surely picked the wrong man to option the Brewer Farm.

"The farmers are Missourian for the most part. They made their little valley bloom, no doubt of that, but surely they should understand that land that could flower like that was worth more than ten dollars an acre, that the Railroad hadn't really promised them in any kind of legal way, anyway."

Williamson confessed to having been in a pickle, for he had deputized Oz Bird.

"There was farmers from miles away, climbing out of sickbeds, swearing it was Buzzard started the shooting, saw it with their own eyes. Amazing how many farmers there was watching that shoot-up. Enough to put Oz Bird away, that is for certain."

....

An hour's ride through cornfields under a sky as silver as zinc brought us to a shed of sun-baked boards with a high loading dock, and an opening on a black, vacant interior. A gray cat crouched frozen at one end of the dock, gazing at us.

"Right here is where it was," Sheriff Williamson said, pointing his whip. "See that kind of newer board there, toward the end of the dock? Right under that ol' cat there. That's newer because Oz Bird's lawyer had the original board prized off there to show the jury two bullet holes in it, prove the local fellows had shot first. But of course there was a dozen that witnessed the other way 'round.

"Buzzard and Gizzard come in a buggy from the livery stable in Custis, and they was here when the farmers come up, all mounted. Buzzard and Gizzard got out, rifle armed, and there was hard words back and forth. Whoever started it, there was a Shiloh of shooting, with four dead and the rest skedaddled. I come out in the morning and found Oz Bird and got him out of there. But the SP Railroad surely let him down flat.

"Now we'll go see Jake Burchard. He'll tell you all about it."

I said I didn't have much sense of Guttman as a participant.

"He was not so hardhead as Buzzard, that was for sure."

Guttman's rifle and duster had been found on the river bank, bearing some blood stains, the sheriff said.

"Did you find out anything about him?" I asked.

"There was an Ike Guttman lived in a boardinghouse on

Second Street in San Francisco. Woman who knew him there said he'd gone back east to visit a sick sister about the time of the shoot-up. Or maybe that was somebody else. Anyway, we couldn't find out any more about him."

We drove on through the lanes in the cornfields to the farmhouse of Jake Burchard, which was set up on a mound, with white clapboards, a tall brick chimney raising a feather of smoke, and a narrow veranda.

....

I sat at a supper of mutton chops, corn, peas, and potatoes with Jake and Mrs. Burchard, she with a face as tight as a fist and gray hair caught into a severe knot at the back of her head, he an open-faced gent of maybe fifty wearing a brown work shirt and laundered blue overalls. Sheriff Williamson had departed, leaving me with the Burchards for the night. I gathered that Jake Burchard's description of the Hungry Valley shoot-out was a local event, and that neighbors would be arriving to sit in on it.

The light was fading as we enjoyed coffee and bread pudding, and an oil lamp on a pulley over the table was lit. A couple of lanky neighbor men, also wearing blue overalls, arrived and were seated. There was talk of the weather, the crops, and the snow pack in the high Sierra whose melt would provide water through the summer and fall.

In the darkness Jake Burchard's face floated over his end of the table, graven with harsh shadows. There were small disturbances as other men, and two women, arrived and seated themselves. I had a curious sensation of being a boy listening in on a men's discussion. I could hear the yipping of coyotes outside at a distance.

Jake Burchard began to speak:

"So we thought we was ready for them if they was to come

and evict Matthew Brewer. We was armed and mounted and ready for them, and we had a patrol like, to watch out for deputies coming in. Henry McDermot had seen to that; Henry had service in the army in the War and knew about drills and sentries and such. We knew they was coming—a man, name of Bird, that was a Wild West Show shooter, and a man name of Guttman. Buzzard and Gizzard. Buzzard had put options in on Brewer's Farm. Bill Williamson had warned us they would be coming."

When he paused for a moment the silence was as intense as a blare of trumpets, and I understood that this was a kind of Homeric recounting of the tale.

He continued, "They come in a buggy rented from Hunters' Livery Stable in Custis, two of them in black hats and long black dusters with their rifles inside their dusters, in that buggy from Hunters' Livery.

"And the Regulators rode up to meet them there at Brewer's cotton shed, and that was a sight like armies drawn up at Bunker Hill, for there was them two out of the carriage in their black hats and dusters, standing there; and there was six of the Regulators mounted up very military: Jed Daughtery and Percy Smith and Hake Feathers and Al Aaronson and Fred Page, and Henry McDermot in his big hat and one hand held up to stop those two highbinders from San Francisco standing there like death all in black like that.

"And Henry said, 'What is your business here, gentlemen?'

"And the Buzzard said, very harsh and certain, 'I have been properly deputized by Sheriff Williamson, and we are here to occupy the farm of one Matthew Brewer, which has been properly reclaimed for nonpayment and contracted to me by the Southern Pacific Railroad.'

"Through all this the Gizzard said not a word, though it

was observed that he was maneuvering his rifle inside his duster.

"And Henry McDermot raised his voice and said, 'No sir, you will do no such thing! And we are here to see you will not!'

"Then the Buzzard said, 'You are in dereliction to the law of California and will suffer accordingly!'

"And all at once he jerked his rifle out from his duster and fired off a shot that knocked Henry McDermot out of the saddle dead, with his dear wife and three childers waiting for him at home."

There was a deep sigh in the darkness all around the table, over which Jake Burchard's pale face hung like a balloon.

"And a second shot that sent Al Aaronson's rifle flying, and him shot in the shoulder, and his little mare horse scampering out of there at a dead run, and the other horses of the Regulators pitching and bucking so nobody could get a fair shot off. Fred Page was shot dead there, with his wife just birthed of a new baby that is eight years old now and never seen her daddy."

This last caused more drawn breaths and sighs from the invisible audience.

"And then, out of the lane, there come galloping Walter Pew on that big white ploughhorse of hissen, shooting as he came, and just then, before he even knew what had happened, Gizzard had run his rifle out and him and Buzzard at the same moment shot Walter out of the saddle. But Walter'd pinked Gizzard!

"There was two dozen more Regulators coming up there, and Buzzard and Gizzard give up trying to get out of there in the buggy from Custis and skittered off into Brewer's cornfield. Nobody felt like chasing them in just then, with all the dead, and Al Aaronson dying, that had to be took to the doc in town, and the sheriff scared up.

"So in the morning Buzzard managed to give himself up to the Sheriff, and Gizzard was never seen again. The river empties into Lake Opalito that has them sinkholes and bad places in it, where the body may be at to this day. His duster was found on the bank there, some blood on it, so surely Gizzard was wounded in the shooting."

"Does anybody remember him?" I inquired.

A bald fellow with a full beard said, "He was just a little fellow, slight like. Clean-shaved. Young. Head shorter than Buz."

"Nothing was found except his duster?"

"Duster and hat and rifle."

"Was there enough water in the river for him to get away down it?"

Baldhead stared at me. He turned to glance at his fellows. No one could remember about that year; some years there was, some there wasn't.

Burchard went on to describe the trial: Buzzard on the stand; the flinching of the Railroad from his defense; the four farmers sent to prison in San Jose for eight months against Buzzard's eight years; the tribulations of the widows and orphaned children, all taken in by neighbors; and the grand day when the four Regulators returned on the train from San Jose—the trees decorated with bunting, the cheers, the hugs, the feast, the speeches.

And now Buzzard was out of prison and had held up the train four stations north of Custis, at Clary, and murdered a railroad guard.

Jake Burchard's recitation went on into the night. It made me think of the *Iliad,* as told by a Trojan.

....

I tried to sleep in a closet of a room upstairs, on a narrow cot, with a pale moon peeking in the window, after ablutions from a big white crockery pitcher and matching bowl. Although the performance was over, I could still hear the stir of the neighbors downstairs. I stared into darkness, reviewing what I had heard.

....

After breakfast, the Burchards' oldest boy, in his shabby overalls, delivered me to the depot in Custis in the spring wagon.

CHAPTER THREE

QUEEN, n. *A woman by whom the realm is ruled when there is a king, and through whom it is ruled when there is not.*
— *The Devil's Dictionary*

FRIDAY, MARCH 11, 1892

Sam Chamberlain, tall and stiffly lean in his fine black broadcloth and with a carnation in his lapel, accompanied a big-bellied man with flowing yellow locks into my office. I surmised that this was Colonel Studely, of the famous Wild West Show. With him was a small woman, her face concealed within a bonnet.

Studely shook hands in a ritualized manner—palms not vertical but turned to the horizontal, with his on top. My hand received a brief muscular squeeze of superiority. He smiled, showing a set of beautiful teeth framed by his mustache.

"Mr. Redmond!"

"Colonel Studely!"

The young woman's face was now visible in her bonnet. She wore a skirt of several yards of fabric and a short jacket, and her waist was cinched by a wide black belt. She was a small woman with a pretty figure. This was Dora Pratt, the celebrated wingshot called the Ace of Shoots, seating herself in the chair Sam Chamberlain swung around for her.

"You have been to call upon Mister Oz Bird, Mr. Redmond!" Colonel Studely said, hooking his thumbs in his belt. We faced each other across my desk, while Sam Chamberlain stood beside Miss Pratt.

"I have read your account in the *Examiner*," Studely continued. "We—" he indicated Miss Pratt— "are interested in any further impressions!"

His eyes were small and sharp and intensely blue, and set unevenly in his broad face, one disconcertingly lower than the other. They were half a degree colder than Oz Bird's.

I told him that Bird had declared himself a vindictive man.

"He threatened my life, did he?"

"Yes, he did." It was gratifying to rattle Colonel Studely's vast self-confidence.

"And Miss Pratt's, as well?"

I met Miss Pratt's steady gaze. "He was more resentful toward you, Colonel Studely."

He folded his arms, stroking his sleeves with his big, ringed hands as he did so. "No doubt the railroad detectives will track him down in good time."

"No doubt," I said.

"Train robbers are given short shrift," Colonel Studely reassured himself. "The Railroad may not be well liked in this state, but it is a powerful force."

"It is that," Sam said.

"Did you encounter any others of his gang?"

"I was blindfolded. One was named Jukes."

Studely squinted his lower eye at me. I thought contempt

and scorn came easily to him, flamboyant, arrogant, roughshod rider that he was. I hoped Oz Bird would give him some sleepless nights.

"Anything you'd like to ask Mr. Redmond, Miss Dory?" the colonel said.

"Not at this juncture," Miss Pratt said in a small, clear voice, rising from her chair with a neat unfolding motion. She cast one expressionless glance back at me as the colonel and Sam Chamberlain led her out of my cubicle.

She returned alone in twenty minutes, slightly flushed and with a lock of darkening fair hair broken loose to curl on her forehead. She had a rosebud of a mouth and high cheekbones that gave her eyes an almost oriental cast.

"Mr. Redmond, I prefer to speak with you alone."

I indicated the chair again, and we sat facing one another.

"I am interested in what Mr. Bird said of me, Mr. Redmond."

"He seems inclined to dispute your divorce, Miss Pratt."

"We were married when I was very young. I owe my career to Mr. Bird, you see."

"So he said."

"We were divorced after he went to prison."

I nodded.

"Did he say that I had had a relation with Colonel Studely?"

I nodded again.

She looked down at her lap. Her gloved hand pushed the errant lock of hair back beneath her bonnet.

"That has long been over," she said. "Mr. Bird is a very jealous man. I had many letters from him from prison."

"To which you did not respond, he said."

She gazed at me for a long moment before she continued. "I was a fair shot with a rifle when I was employed by Texas Jack's Combination. Mr. Bird helped me to become a very good shot."

She sighed. "I am grateful to him, but our life was not a happy one. I was much relieved to be free of him."

I felt a sudden, queer urge to protect her, which surprised me.

"He said he had hoped to acquire the Brewer Farm so that you and he could change your lives."

Her lips parted and compressed. "Yes, he had mentioned such a notion. It was his plan to cease his career as an exhibition shooter."

"But it was not your notion?"

She shook her head, her face turned down.

"He said you would be accompanying him to 'points south,' whatever that means."

I heard her intake of breath. "He has a connection in Argentina," she whispered.

"He seemed certain you would come with him."

"He is a murderer, Mr. Redmond!"

Indeed he was.

"Colonel Studely has planned a grand parade for the Show?" I asked.

"On Sunday afternoon. There are a hundred and fourteen of us."

"Shooting off guns?"

"That is part of it. Cowboys and Indians, a stagecoach. Ropers, riders, cowgirls. There are several of us exhibition shootists."

"The police will be aware of danger," I said.

"Yes." She rose. "Thank you, Mr. Redmond." She removed the glove from her small hand, which she extended to me.

I bent over it. Her eyes were brown, with darker flecks. They were warm eyes. She smelled of lilac. When she went out the door, I admired the small shape of her. I had a curious feeling of having been drawn into a net, not by a spider, but by a small but perfectly capable creature.

The *Examiner* headlines the next day read

BIRD HUNT

....

OSWALD BIRD SOUGHT STATEWIDE

....

PEACE OFFICERS OF CALIFORNIA ON THE WATCH

....

SATURDAY, MARCH 12, 1892

Saturday evening, Bierce having returned from Auburn, we trod the Cocktail Route together. The Yellowstone Bar on Montgomery Street was our favorite, with its warm saloon democracy of after-work drinkers, the place illuminated by gasoliers and the phosphorescent, plump, white limbs of the smiling beauties in the paintings on the wall, reflected in the mirrors behind the bar. On display was a vast stock of foodstuffs.

A young man approached Bierce with his jaw thrust out and a fervent eye: "Mr. Bierce, can you advise your readers on the relation between the sexes?"

Bierce casually blew out his breath. "Young man," he said, "I believe a horizontal surface is best. And I recommend room temperature."

The young man stared after us as we progressed toward the food layouts.

An older, red-faced man with a pink flower in his lapel and a plate of food in his hand bowed to Bierce, and asked when he might be heard from on the new subject of Eugenics.

"When I have in fact informed myself on the subject," Bierce said, returning the bow.

Seated, with our plates before us, he with a glass of bourbon and I with a lager, Bierce formally complimented me on the Bird interview and on the account of my trip to Hungry Valley.

"No doubt Bird wished to speak with an *Examiner* journalist because of the *Examiner*'s well-known—and well-justified—opposition to the Railroad," he said.

My effort had been to be neutral in regard to the facts, but Sam Chamberlain's editing had focused the blame on the Southern Pacific Railroad, which was *Examiner* policy. The piece would please Oswald Bird.

"Tomorrow Colonel Studely's Wild West Show will parade down Market Street," I said, and described the danger facing Colonel Studely.

"You think there is a possibility he will be shot out of the saddle?" Bierce asked.

"The police will be on guard, and of course he has his own prize shootists, including the Ace of Shoots."

"The possibility of a gun battle between Bad Bird and Little Miss Nevermiss!" Bierce said. "Perhaps I will attend. She is Colonel Studely's paramour, is she?"

"Is no longer, she said."

The usual squad of sycophants had gathered around Bierce, and he took the opportunity to discourse on the improbable to them: "Nothing is so improbable as what is true," he said, rather pompously, I thought. "It is the unexpected that occurs; but that is not saying enough; it is also the unlikely—one might also say the impossible. The ragged convict escaped from the prison in Constantinople may not marry the royal princess in fiction, but he may in real life!"

We made an arrangement to attend the parade together, and I left Bitter Bierce to his admirers.

SUNDAY, MARCH 13, 1892

The *Sunday Examiner* flourished more headlines of Oz Bird, who may have been sighted in Sacramento.

In his column, Bierce attacked a Miss Augusta Frayn of the Pacific Coast Women's Press Association, who had had the temerity to address a reproach to him:

"Miss Frayn of the Press Association shows distinct signs of aggression, and I confess the necessity and obligation of saying something in defense of the Maker for permitting me to exist.

" 'We welcome criticism,' Miss Frayn says, 'deprecate being burlesqued, and resist being misrepresented.' This is a very proper spirit, but every male critic knows that the kind of criticism which women welcome has not yet been invented."

On the same page, Miss Keith's women's column included an attack on the medicine Calomel, which was much prescribed by fashionable doctors for female complaints:

"Why, pray, would the earnest, presumably wise practitioner, who considers himself a scientist, prescribe for his patients—especially those of the weaker gender—a medicine produced from a deadly metal well known as such to the mining fraternity: mercurous chloride, Calomel? Mercurous chloride is known to kill insects, it poisons small animals, and it most certainly hastened the demise of the distinguished novelist Miss Louisa May Alcott."

Miss Keith concluded with the following quatrain:

"And when I must resign my breath
Pray let me die a natural death
And bid the world that long farewell
Without one dose of Cal-o-mel!"

Bierce and I took a stand among the crowd of spectators on the corner of Geary Street to watch Colonel Studely's Wild West Show approach east down Market Street, accompanied by a brass band whose out-of-tempo thumping and tootling settled down as it drew nearer. Occasionally, up the street, there would be a volley of blank cartridge fire, Comanche yells, and the shouts of cowboys.

Colonel Studely led the way, astride a tall white horse. His shock of yellow hair and sweeping mustache were the color of his horse's mane, which gave the curious impression that they were a single animal. He waved his hat right and left in a royal manner. He wore immaculate white buckskins and his chest was decorated with four medals with colorful ribbons, no doubt awarded him by the crowned heads of Europe. He was a grand figure, preceding his associates and the brass band with the sun glinting off the instruments, the drum booming, the bass horn grunting. I saw Bierce frowning at him with dislike.

Two yards behind and to one side of Studely rode Miss Pratt, on an Indian pony. She was, curiously, dressed as a schoolgirl, in a broad hat, white blouse, black skirt, stockings, and low boots. She carried her rifle in an upright position, resting on her left thigh. There were cheers for the Colonel, for her, and for the Ponca chieftain Short Bear, who rode to the right of her. He also wore buckskins, and a headdress of gleaming feathers atop a dark brown, sour, wrinkled old face with an undershot jaw like a barracuda's. He also carried his rifle balanced on his leg, and a brace of knives was thrust into his belt, for he was a famous knife thrower. The main body of the Show's performers followed the band, straggling out at a considerable distance behind their leader.

A quartet of Stetsoned gentlemen in buckskins, city clothing, and combinations thereof rode in the rank behind the colonel. One of these wore a fantastical Mexican hat much laden with silver embroidery, and rode in such a flamboyant style as to catch every eye. The paving stones rang beneath the hoof irons.

I waved at Miss Pratt, who responded by waggling her rifle

barrel at me. Colonel Studely continued to fling his hat out right and left as he led his regiment down Market Street.

The riders rattled on past Bierce and me: stone-faced Indians sporting feathered headdresses; cowboys in full regalia; a quartet of cowgirls in buckskins, waving; mountain men in coonskin caps; an old Concord coach with gesticulating men hanging out of its windows; a squadron of men in civilian clothing, flourishing broad-brimmed hats. There were cheers and whistles from the crowd gathered along the sidewalks of Market Street.

The band began to play a march, and all at once cowboys and Indians whipped out rifles and sidearms and assaulted the sky with the racket of their shooting and yelling. Smoke drifted up between the buildings.

Up ahead there came a moan from the spectators, and a different kind of shout. Bierce clutched my arm. A red bandanna had appeared, plastered to Colonel Studely's buckskin back. He was leaning forward over his horse's neck. He slipped sideways, recovered himself, slipped again. I saw then that it was not a red bandanna on his back, but his blood. He fell.

CHAPTER FOUR

GUILT, n. *The condition of one who is known to have committed an indiscretion, as distinguished from the state of him who has covered his tracks.*
— *The Devil's Dictionary*

SUNDAY, MARCH 13, 1892

In the confusion that followed the shooting of Colonel Studely, I pushed my way through the lurching, noisy, and deadly silent crowd to where Miss Pratt sat on her Indian pony. The police would be searching the streets and adjacent buildings for Oz Bird, in disguise or not, who might well be making his way to his ex-wife to spirit her off to "points south."

"Come with me, Miss Pratt!" I called up to her. She gave me a dazed look, handed me her rifle, and slid out of her saddle, presenting the reins to the young fellow mounted next to her, who wore a shirt decorated with an array of gleaming buttons.

My arm around her, I pressed our way to the corner of Geary, where Bierce joined us. The three of us hurried to Montgomery street, and the *Examiner* building, Miss Pratt walking silently between us with her head down. I still carried her rifle.

In Bierce's office she slumped in a chair, a pathetic figure in her schoolgirl costume, her flat hat at a tilt, her face so white it made her lips seem preternaturally red. She sat stiffly in her chair with her arms resting on its arms. Bierce sent for Sam Chamberlain, who along with Willie Hearst was often in the building on Sundays. Miss Pratt cut her eyes at Sam as he entered, then resumed staring at the skull on Bierce's desk. I thought of Oz Bird's insistence that she was his wife.

Bierce described the assassination to Sam Chamberlain.

"Where did Bird shoot him from?" Sam wanted to know.

Oz Bird must have shot Studely from a window in one of the buildings along Market Street, or from the crowd along the sidewalk. I recalled Studely sitting erect in the saddle, waving left and right.

"Robbie—*fell!*" Miss Pratt whispered, straightening her childish hat. "Robbie, falling from a saddle! He just—*fell!*

"I assume there is some second-in-command," Sam said, leaning forward so as to be on the same level as her face. "Someone in charge of finances, so the Show can go on?"

"Mr. Boxcroft. Percy Radley is in Cincinnati, arranging engagements. There are many engagements ..." Her voice trailed off.

"Bird announced his intention to shoot the colonel!" Sam said, squinting at me.

"He did that," I said.

"On the other hand, " Bierce said, retiring to seat himself behind his desk, "was it not a perfect opportunity for someone else to commit murder?"

"There is a Mrs. Dierdorf in Denver who should be notified," Miss Pratt said suddenly.

"A relative or a relation?" Sam asked.

She looked at him blankly.

"Miss Pratt," Bierce said, "who were the riders in the rank with you just behind the colonel?"

She shook her head once as though to clear it and then fixed her gaze on him. She hesitated before she spoke, maybe considering whether Bierce had the right to ask the question. Then she said, moving her hand to establish the order, "Me, Billy Buttons, Short Bear, Enrique Garza, Mr. Boxcroft—the lawyer—and Darkey Duncan."

"Your rank did not engage in shooting blanks along with the main body behind the band?"

She shook her head.

Sam said, "Oz Bird—"

Bierce interrupted. "Sam, it does not seem to me possible that Studely was shot from a window along the parade route, nor that the shot came from someone in the main body, which was at some distance back. I was there. I was watching the colonel. I think the shot came from directly behind."

"There are commitments in Seattle and Denver!" Miss Pratt said, moving her hand to her hat as if to hold it on.

"Miss Pratt," Bierce said gently, "to whom does the ownership of the Show now pass?"

Again she took a long moment to respond. "There's someone in Iowa, a half brother."

"Has Oz Bird been in touch with you, Miss Pratt?" Sam wanted to know.

"No, he has not!" Rising, she said, "I would like to go to my hotel now, please!"

Sam raised an eyebrow at me. I moved to take her arm and picked up her rifle, which I had leaned against the desk. "I will accompany you there, Miss Pratt."

I escorted her outside and hailed a hack—Tom Redmond with the Ace of Shoots of Colonel Studely's Wild West Show, a silent, frightened young woman in a child's dress leaning her head against my shoulder, her rifle barrel prodding my leg. I felt a sense of involuntary involvement again.

"Poor Robbie," she whispered. "How a gun will have its prey! How—" She halted herself.

I muttered something about the terrible shock.

When we drew up before her hotel, she said, "Thank you for bringing me here, Mr. Redmond. I'm afraid I am not very sensible, just now."

I helped her out of the hack and into the lighted doorway, past the fancily dressed doorman. The young man with the panel of buttons on his shirtfront, who had been mounted next to Miss Pratt in the parade, leaped up from a chair, exclaiming, "Miss Dory!"

"I am safe now, Mr. Redmond, thank you," Miss Pratt said.

I handed the rifle to button-shirt, bowed, and departed.

....

When I returned, Sam and Bierce were in Willie Hearst's office, already in conference with the editor and proprietor of the *Examiner* as well as chief of detectives Dan O'Brien, a tall man with a creased scowl of a face outlined by a fringe of beard.

Chief O'Brien, with whom I had already had a long interview concerning Bird, scowled at me as though he had forgotten my name. He stood with his hands clasped behind his back and showed no interest in touching palms.

"Any revelations from the Ace of Shoots?" Sam wanted to know. Willie Hearst gazed at me from behind his desk, his face young and narrow beneath his center-parted hair.

"She is distraught," I said.

"I will have a talk with that lady," Chief O'Brien said. "Has she heard from Bird, I wonder?"

"She said she has not," I said.

"Mr. Bierce maintains that Bird could not have shot Colonel Studely from a window along the way," Willie Hearst said to O'Brien.

O'Brien raised his eyebrows. "Hid out among the pack of

them firing at the sky? Or part of the crowd? Nobody's come forward. What's he look like, mister?"

"Medium height," I said. "Medium everything. Short growth of beard."

He regarded me expressionlessly. He said, "I understand Studely and Miss Pratt was domiciled together."

"She informed me that that has long been over," I said. "She spoke of a Mrs. Dierdorf in Denver."

"No fury like a woman cast off, the way I see it," O'Brien said.

I felt impelled to defend Miss Pratt, understanding police mentality enough to know that it would latch on to the most logical suspect. I said I had handled Miss Pratt's rifle immediately after the shot, and had determined from the lack of heat that it had not been fired.

"I also tested it in my office," Bierce said.

"You're the only one here that's met with Bird," O'Brien said to me in an accusing tone. "Said he was going to shoot the colonel and that Potter SP fellow, didn't he?"

"And take Miss Pratt with him," I said.

"Ha!"

"Will you and Mr. Redmond participate in this investigation on the part of the *Examiner,* Mr. Bierce?" Willie Hearst asked.

"If Chief O'Brien will not consider us an interference."

The *Examiner*'s reporters often acted as detectives, "Giving Justice a lift when her chariot gets bogged down," as Willie liked to say. He had written editorially: "*Examiner* reporters are everywhere; they are the first to see everything, and the first to perceive the true meaning of what they see. Whether a child is to be found, an eloping girl to be brought home, or a murder to be traced, one of our staff is sure to give the sleepy detectives their first pointers . . ."

"Glad of help," O'Brien said, not entirely convincingly. "I

have got twenty detectives looking out for Oz Bird. And every patrolman in town is on the watch now, too. In disguise maybe! Maybe they have laid hands on him already."

He said to Bierce, "I will consider it that Colonel Studely was shot by Oz Bird until I see evidence otherwise." He said to me, "Better keep an eye on Miss Pratt, I reckon."

"Yes!"

As the chief of detectives, Sam, Bierce, and I filed out of Willie Hearst's office, O'Brien said to Bierce, "Gents in that second row was mostly some kind of fancy shooters, is that what you mean?"

"That is what I mean, Chief O'Brien," Bierce said.

CHAPTER FIVE

INNOCENCE, n. *The state or condition of a criminal whose counsel has fixed the jury.*

— *The Devil's Dictionary*

MONDAY, MARCH 14, 1892

The San Francisco police had failed to lay hands on Oswald Bird after the shooting, and in the morning I took a horsecar to the Southern Pacific Railroad headquarters on Townsend Street, from where many believed the state of California was governed. Arliff K. Potter was a vice president with a second-story office.

Two helmeted patrolmen were on duty in the lobby, one lounging against a magazine stand, the other pacing. I caught a glimpse of the great capitalist himself, Collis P. Huntington, in a monkey jacket and striped trousers. His head had a curious shape, which Bierce had described as the dromedary bumps of cupidity and self-esteem. Huntington clapped a stovepipe hat over these, and was gone in a flurry of lackeys.

I tramped up a flight of stairs and found another patrolman standing beside the door that bore Potter's name. I identified myself and was admitted. Arliff K. Potter rose from behind an important desk as I came in. He was a short man with some twenty-five strands of colorless hair combed across his freckled scalp. He advanced a step to meet me.

"Mr. Redmond?"

"Mr. Potter?"

We touched hands. He motioned me to a straight chair facing the desk, and retreated behind it. "Cigar?" he said, proffering.

I thanked him no, and brought out my notebook and pencil.

"You have been threatened by Oswald Bird, Mr. Potter."

He managed a dignified nod, and stroked a pale hand over the strands of hair.

"Does this frighten you, sir? Colonel Studely has been murdered."

"I am well protected, as you see, Mr. Redmond." He gestured. "Every patrolman in the City is on the lookout for Oswald Bird. There will be a reward."

"Would you recognize him?"

"I'm afraid not." He folded his arms, still standing. "I had very little contact with the fellow, despite his claims." He launched into a spiel as to the SP's lack of culpability in the Hungry Valley tragedy, which I interrupted.

"The Railroad's association with Bird and Guttman was entered into because they were marksmen?"

Potter produced a petulant frown. "Mr. Redmond, as I recall, it was *Bird* who came to *me* with a proposition. I was then in charge of certain land transactions by the Railroad."

"He proposed to contract for a settler's property the SP had foreclosed upon?"

"That is correct, Mr. Redmond."

"Bird and Guttman were prepared for opposition when they went to take possession of the farm?"

"There had been threats and denouncements against them."

"Buzzard and Gizzard," I said.

An eruption took place in his face; I recognized it as an expression of dampened humor. "I believe those appellations were used to malign them," he said.

I made a show of consulting my notes. "You may have seen my interview with Bird in the *Examiner* a week ago. Bird told me that you made an arrangement for him to option the Brewer Farm and saw to it that he was deputized by the sheriff there. But, after the shooting, the Railroad claimed it was in no way involved in his actions."

Potter said, "Is it not reasonable to believe that a murderer such as Bird would relate events in a manner that places him in the best light?"

"Why was Bird deputized?"

"Mr. Redmond, the foreclosure of the Brewer Farm was a legal action."

"The sheriff was pleased enough to stay out of that action?"

"I believe he had other responsibilities at the time."

"Tell me about Isaac Guttman."

"As I recall, he was an associate of Bird's. I knew nothing about him. I knew only that Bird was a Wild West Show entertainer."

"What happened to Guttman?"

"I would think you would have asked that of Bird, who was surely the last to see him. You must be familiar with the transcript of the trial, Mr. Redmond; much of it saw print in the *Call*. I believe it was assumed that Guttman drowned while trying to escape, or that he fled the state so as not to be apprehended like his partner."

"And not to be defended by the Railroad like his partner," I said.

He frowned at me severely.

·················

The afternoon headlines read

BIRD SOUGHT BY PLAINCLOTHESMEN

·····································

DETECTIVES ON THE TRAIL

·····································

CHIEF VOWS EVERY EFFORT

·····································

At his desk, Bierce, guarded by the chalk-white skull, brandished a sheet of paper on which names were listed.

"The rank behind Studely," he said. "Those close behind him had the clearest shot at their leader. Then came the band, then the main body. I would think it too long a shot from the main body. I also very much doubt the possibility of Oz Bird concealed in a Market Street frontage. I have information of the rank from Mr. Boxcroft, the Show's lawyer, who has assumed command. It matches Miss Pratt's."

He read from the list:

"Left to right: first Miss Pratt, then a trick rider named Billy Buttons, who is devoted to Miss Pratt. As is the Ponca chief, Short Bear, who was next. He is Miss Pratt's especial protector— her familiar, in the sense of a protective spirit. She is the only one who can deal with him when he becomes morose, which is often. He repays her with total allegiance. Buttons is also a shootist, although fancy riding is more his specialty.

"The Mexican with the big hat is Enrique Garza. He is much admired for his accomplishments. Boxcroft says that he can do everything in the cowboy metier better than North American cowboys can. He is an exotic fellow, very popular with the ladies and usually encumbered with several of them. Next to him was Boxcroft.

"The rider farthest right is also an exotic. Darkey Duncan. He is a Negro, a world's champion bulldogger, and is known to subdue his prey with both hands raised, as he was witness to a bulldog-and-bull conflict in England, in which the bulldog got his teeth into the bull's lower lip and quieted the animal right down. Duncan has adopted this technique, if we can believe such a thing. Leaps from his horse to the bull's back, all at full speed across the arena—grasps the horns, and digs his heels into the earth to bring the animal down. Then he clenches the bull's lip between his teeth and raises his hands in victory. He is very popular.

"Those are the chief performers. There are some hundred other, lesser lights, including four so-called cowgirls and two Chinese cooks. The Combination—a word they use to refer to the Show—is encamped south of the City on the big flats along the Bay, adjacent to the Fairgrounds, where we must look into these interesting suspects."

He sat back in his chair, fingers tented, a smug expression on his face. "And I have had my first taste of Miss Keith," he said.

"Nose-pincher glasses and lips like razors?"

"She is not unattractive. She is a lecturer, however, as one may suspect from her Sunday column. I have been lectured on the historical excellence of the female gender."

I saw that the lecture was to be passed along to me, no doubt in scornful terms. But he was respectful enough.

"It seems," he proceeded, "that women were the founders of society, despite their bondage to the male. Women created culture. They have given us coordination and cooperation. They domesticated animals, they invented weaving and textiles in general—the first dimension of civilization. They were the first ceramic artisans; they developed the forms, techniques, and uses of pottery. They first conceived of the idea of shelter for themselves and their helpless infants. They invented dyes, the arts of decoration and beauty. Women had a hand in creating religion—to their sorrow, as Miss Keith points out. They also deserve credit for the civilization of the male."

"Well," I said, uncertain what my response should be.

"And I have an inkling!" he said, raising one finger as a marker. "I believe that she is a poetess!"

Too bad for Miss Keith, I thought.

....

The next day's Bird headline read

SP ANNOUNCES REWARD

....

$2,000 FOR BIRD, DEAD OR ALIVE

....

SP HOPES TO CLAIM ITS OWN REWARD

....

There followed an interview with the Railroad's chief detective, Bartholomew M. Culver, that was all bluster and no content.

At ten o'clock in the morning, Bierce and I took a hack to the Fairgrounds.

CHAPTER SIX

LITERALLY, adv. *Figuratively, as: "The pond was literally full of fish";
"The ground was literally alive with snakes"; etc.*
— *The Devil's Dictionary*

TUESDAY, MARCH 15, 1892

On the siding, lined up like a file of rusted elephants, were
the ten or twelve freight cars that had transported Colonel
Studely's Wild West Show from its last booking. Beyond were
the Fairgrounds, on lowlands beside the Bay. A high fence had
been erected, but the gate was open. Bierce paid the hackie and
we stepped through the gate, into a scene of activity. A water
wagon with a round tank on its bed rolled past, spraying crystal
streams on the dry ground. Beyond I could see a figure standing
on a horse's back, rifle to her cheek, aiming as the brown pony
bore her, swaying, at a flowing trot. Dora Pratt wore a gray
dress and bonnet, aiming but not firing as the pony carried her
along. I could not think how she could keep her footing, much
less her balance, much less her aim.

"That is quite astonishing!" Bierce said.

Other horses were also in motion, a team of them dragging
the Concord coach with faces at the window, another at a swift

gallop, with a cowboy leaning out of his saddle so far he was head down, sweeping a gauntleted hand at something on the bare ground. Dust rose from the hooves, and there was a steady whiff of it in the air.

Bierce halted to gaze after Miss Pratt in her fast trot.

The Mexican in his big silvered hat rode a white horse that bucked to its back legs, walked that way for several steps, and then plunged forward to all four and into a quick gallop before being pulled by the rider up to two legs again. Farther over was a crowd of feather-headdressed Indians and sombreroed cowboys trotting along together, a couple of them with cigars in their jaws like bowsprits. Two cowgirls trotted off to one side, one of them flipping her hat in the air and catching it with a graceful stretch. I could hear the shards of their laughter from where I stood at the gate.

The Wild West Show, which had canceled several performances in deference to its proprietor's death, was rehearsing.

Beyond the crowd of cowboys and Indians was a large corrugated-metal barn that must have been carried in one of the freight cars and reassembled at the Fairgrounds, and a vast enclosure of horses with tossing heads.

Bierce and I moved along inside the fence so as not to be run down by the performers in their activities. Dora Pratt saw us and trotted over, lowering herself into the saddle. Her pony halted, and she slipped to the ground beside us.

"Hullo, Mr. Bierce, Mr. Redmond! Come to see us in action?"

"We have been watching you in action with admiration, Miss Pratt," Bierce said.

"How can you stand in the saddle and pretend to shoot anything?" I asked.

The twitch of her lips reminded me of how rare her smiles were. She wore a black band on her upper arm. In answer to my question, she indicated the slots built into her saddle where she could slip the toes of her shoes. She stowed her rifle in its scabbard, slung alongside.

"If you would, introduce us to some of your fellow performers, Miss Pratt," Bierce said.

One of the other riders was already approaching. This was the trick rider Billy Buttons, with the array of buttons sewn to his shirtfront.

Bierce was introduced, and the four of us walked together, leading the two horses to the "Jacal," a shelter roofed with boards whose interstices let through lines of sunlight in which dust motes circulated. We sat on benches at a table there. Dora Pratt explained to Buttons that Ambrose Bierce and I were writing news articles on the murder of Colonel Studely for the San Francisco *Examiner*.

"Well, Oz said he was gone to do it!" Billy Buttons said in admiration, waving his hand through a sheet of sunlight. He was a lean, mustached fellow with a growth of beard on his cheeks and something peculiar abut his eyes. He focused on me. "Was it you wrote that piece about going up to see him?"

I nodded. "Did you know him?"

"Did! I was in the Show when he was in it."

"Before Oz went to prison," Miss Pratt said.

Bierce said, "You are convinced that Bird fired the shot, Mr. Buttons?"

"Tell you, if Oz put out that he would shoot Rob Studely, he done it! Get away with it, too!" Buttons folded his arms on his chest and regarded us brightly.

"How would he have accomplished it?"

"Put on a big hat and a Hallowe'en nose—and banged away!"

"What is this about, Mr. Bierce?" Dora Pratt wanted to know.

"It may be that someone else took the opportunity to do away with the colonel, you see, Miss Pratt."

She gazed back at Bierce with her chin up. Buttons looked puzzled.

The Indian chief, in a greasy denim coverall and with a single eagle feather in his headband, approached us. Miss Pratt flicked her fingers at his sleeve as he passed her to seat himself. He scowled across the table at Billy Buttons, and then squinted at Bierce and me. The hafts of three bowie knives were docked in a kind of apron.

Miss Pratt introduced us to Short Bear.

"How!" the Ponca chief said in the approved Indian manner.

"Are we to understand that everyone in the Show mourns Colonel Studely?" I said.

Short Bear emitted a grunt that was surely a laugh.

"I'm afraid that is not the case, Mr. Redmond," Miss Pratt said sadly.

"Everybody hated his guts!" Billy Buttons said.

Indeed, there did not seem to be much sign of grief for Colonel Studely, aside from the black band on Miss Pratt's arm.

The rider in the Mexican hat thundered up on his white horse and crashed to a halt. Garza dismounted and seated himself at our table, all in one sleek, graceful motion. He seemed to relax instantly, as though he had been lounging there for an hour, presenting his round, brown, mustachioed, smiling face to each in turn. Miss Pratt introduced him as "Reeky."

"You have come to write historia of famous Wild West rider Enrique Garza!" he said. "How it is overdue, senores!"

Miss Pratt regarded him amiably, Short Bear with his chin out, and Billy Buttons with an expression of impatience. Bierce gazed from face to face.

"These gents is inquiring who of us do not mourn Rob Studely," Buttons said. "How about you, Reek?"

"I mourn, I mourn!"

With some slight movement of her head, Miss Pratt's face was illuminated by one of the sheets of sunlight piercing the planks of the roof, and I realized that she was beautiful. More than that, I perceived that it was her effort *not* to appear beautiful, her pale cameo face always cased in her bonnet or hidden beneath her schoolgirl straw. Just as suddenly, her bonneted countenance drew back out of the sun ray and she again became the rather mousy presence, who was one of the world's great female exhibition shooters. And I considered again that strong protective instinct that she had engendered in me.

"I do not have the advantage of having met Colonel Studely," Bierce commented, "but in the parade, which I witnessed, he did seem a rather arrogant presence."

"Mean to Missy Acey Shoots!" Short Bear growled.

"Never mind it, Short Bear!" Miss Pratt said.

"Miss Dory is the best wingshot there is, and I mean Annie Oakley," Billy Buttons said, leaning forward earnestly. "She was not treated as such!"

"Enough, please!" Miss Pratt said. She sat with her hands clasped together on the table before her.

"You will not quit on us, Missy Dory?" Garza said.

"I will not quit on you, Reeky," she said, and her hand reached out to touch his gauntleted wrist.

"We will quit together! We will ride to Mexico! To the sweet valleys of Michoacán!"

"She is staying right here," Billy Buttons said.

"Missy Dory make sun come up, Mister white-eye!" Short Bear said to Bierce.

I said, "Bird said that he and Miss Pratt were going to quit the Show and go to farming in Tulare County eight or nine years ago."

"That was never my intention!" Miss Pratt said.

Bierce wanted to know if all present had been in the Show when Bird was in it. Only Buttons raised a hand. "I was. Boxy was."

Another rider drew up and dismounted. This was the large black man Darkey Duncan, wearing a red bandanna bound over his head like a pirate and with the undershot jaw of the bulldog whose bull-baiting methods he had copied; the resemblance was comical.

His dark eyes, shot with yellow, appraised Bierce and me. "Newspaper hands," he said. "You the one went to see Oz Bird?" he said to me. "You tell him he shows up here, he will leave boots first! Hear?"

He brushed past Miss Pratt to seat himself beyond Garza, his big hand on the table like a dark lobster claw.

Boxcroft, the Show's lawyer, also arrived, dismounting to shake hands with Bierce and me. "Welcome to Colonel Studely's Wild West, gentlemen! What a tragedy he is not here to welcome you himself!"

He was tall and slightly stooped, with patent-leather hair of a brilliant blackness and a wisp of a mustache. He regarded Bierce worriedly, but with a cast of presumption that, through us, the Wild West Show would gain newspaper recognition and, consequently, ticket sales.

"Miss Pratt has graciously introduced us to her fellow performers," Bierce said.

"We are struck dumb by this tragic event!" Boxcroft said. "Oz Bird!" He glanced around him as though to summon evidence of struck-dumbedness, or else, I thought, to insist upon it.

"You are convinced the assassin was Bird?" Bierce asked.

"Who else would it be?"

"That is what we are here to learn. Did Colonel Studely have enemies in the Show?"

"All of us!" Darkey Duncan said.

The lawyer managed a laugh. "But what a handsome figure he was, booted, spurred, and mounted! Honored by monarchs! Medals on his breast!"

"Mean as a skunk!" Billy Buttons said.

Miss Pratt looked stern. "Robbie put this Combination together," she said. "He made it one of the best shows in the country. He held it together!"

"She is a loyal person," Billy Buttons said to me.

Short Bear made a gesture with his right hand, as if jamming a knife into something above us.

"Oz Bird!" Darkey Duncan pronounced, his arms folded across his chest. He glared from Bierce to me. "We will be on watch for him, Newspape!"

But surely only Miss Pratt, Boxcroft, and Billy Buttons would know Bird by sight, I thought.

"Come with me, gentlemen!" Boxcroft said to Bierce and me. "Let us adjourn to Robbie's big tent."

Miss Pratt looked me in the eye but did not smile. Hands were shaken again as we took our leave of the Ace of Shoots and her fellow performers, and, following Boxcroft, who led his horse, started across the arena.

"They are her courtiers!" Bierce whispered to me. "Her guard. Her Praetorians! Did you see that she managed to touch each one of them? All but our host here, that is."

CHAPTER SEVEN

LAWYER, n. *One skilled in circumvention of the law.*
— The Devil's Dictionary

TUESDAY, MARCH 15, 1892

Colonel Studely's big tent was like a storeroom containing mementos of many lands: Turkish rugs covering the floor, elaborate folding chairs that must have come from the English Army in India, bright circles of hanging brass platters, and a gleaming brass canopied bedstead half-exposed behind curtains. I grimaced to think of Dora Pratt occupying that bed.

A parrot was a tall slash of green and yellow on a polished wood stand.

Lawyer Boxcroft folded his arms and stood looking around him, his mouth set in a downward slant.

"Rocks and shoals!" the parrot called out, surveying me with one eye, then the other.

"Well, Mr. Boxcroft," Bierce said with an encompassing flick of his hand. "To whom does all this now belong?"

"Complicated," Boxcroft said. "There's a relative of Robbie's in Iowa. Des Moines. About as much interest in the Show as a trip to the moon."

"What about Miss Pratt?"

"Complicated," Boxcroft said again.

"How is that, Mr. Boxcroft?"

Boxcroft appeared to be conferring with himself, scowling. He uncoupled his arms and rubbed his hands together. "Mr. Bierce, I can tell you that there is a case for common-law marriage. Robbie and Miss Pratt were what can certainly be called man and wife for long enough, even though they separated, bed and breakfast, last year. Required is some evidence that Robbie thought of himself and Dora as man and wife."

"And that is a problem as to the ownership of the Show?"

"That is correct." With a cock of his patent-leather head, he added, "The actual physical equipment of the Show does not amount to much. Nor is Miss Pratt of a combative nature," he added.

"Are there other women?" Bierce inquired.

"There are. There were. There is a lady in Denver."

"Mrs. Dierdorf," I said.

Boxcroft scowled at Bierce. They both scowled at me. I stepped over to a metal sale rack of photographs. One was of Studely on a rearing horse, waving his hat; another showed the Ponca chief in a magnificent headdress. There were photographs of riders; bulldoggers; the Concord coach, laden with passengers; Billy Buttons grinning down at a mutt dog that grinned back up at him; Dora Pratt as a schoolgirl, standing with her rifle, backed by four tall gents—the black man, Billy Buttons, Short Bear (with arms folded), and big-hatted Enrique Garza. I extracted one of these to study it more closely.

"That's a handsome parrot, Mr. Boxcroft," Bierce observed.

"His name is Ted. He is a fine fellow; aren't you, Ted? Given to Robbie by an admirer in Elmira, New York, many years ago."

"Where's Dory?" the bird said.

"She'll be along soon, Ted!"

"We gather that the colonel was not universally loved by his employees," Bierce said.

"That is true, sir."

"Miss Pratt seems to have been unappreciated," I said.

"Appreciated a good deal at one time!" Boxcroft said, his face contorting into a wink that made me want to punch him in the mouth.

"Up until when?" Bierce said.

"Most of a year ago. April. There was a big blowout, and Miss Pratt moved out of this tent. As we have said, Robbie had other female friends here and there. I did not see that there would be any legal ramifications."

"Was the blowout about other women?"

Boxcroft's face screwed up comically. "It was a fuss over Billy's dog, in fact. Billy had a crippled mutt dog he loved to distraction. Named Threepo. Robbie made Billy take him out and shoot him. There was a grand fracas over that; everybody got into it. I thought the Combination was going to blow up right there."

"Threepo?" Bierce said.

"Three-legged," Boxcroft said. "Robbie couldn't stand the sight of Threepo around. He hated the sight of anything ugly. He was a devotee of the new science of Eugenics, you see. Which made his contempt for all he disapproved the more potent. I exercised what talents I have as a diplomatist, and in the end everybody calmed down. The show must go on! But that's when Dory moved out."

"Where's Dory?" the parrot demanded, sidling on his perch.

Boxcroft's face screwed up again, not comically this time. "She had put up with that philandering, blackmailing, parsimonious fraud for seven years!"

"Blackmail?" Bierce inquired.

"Robbie liked to have something on everyone," Boxcroft said. He looked as though he wished the subject had not come up.

"On yourself, as well?" Bierce wanted to know.

Boxcroft laughed. "Not much there, sir!"

"What did he have against Miss Pratt?"

"Something to do with Oz Bird, no doubt. You must understand that it was impossible to fathom the complexities and degree of Robbie Studely's suspicions."

"We would be pleased if you would elaborate, Mr. Boxcroft," Bierce said.

"Oz was a wretch and a scoundrel; no knowing what he might have involved her in. And I am afraid I have elaborated too much already!"

"Rocks and shoals!" Ted called out again.

"Miss Pratt had bad luck with men," I said. "But I see she is much beloved here."

"Short Bear believes she is some kind of Indian deity," Boxcroft said. "And Billy Buttons would lay down his life for her. Trick riders tend to be crazy as coots, and about as reliable."

"Duncan spouts threats against Oz Bird," I said.

"He is a man to make good on his threats!" Boxcroft said, with another short laugh. "But one must wonder if Dory does not still have a yen for bad old Oz! She *did* dote on him once."

"Bird told Mr. Redmond that he had optioned the Brewer Farm so he and Miss Pratt could quit the show and take up farming," Bierce said.

Boxcroft shrugged. "Oz was on his way out, and Dory already on her road to glory. You can understand that he might've wanted to retire, but *she* didn't!"

His words echoed what Dora Pratt had said.

And just then, Miss Pratt appeared, entering the room with

head-lowered diffidence, nodding to Boxcroft as she passed him. The parrot tramped up and down to see her, and she moved toward him and slipped him a cracker from her skirt pocket.

"Where's Dory?" he said excitedly.

"Right here, Teddy!"

"Ted does love his lady-friend!" Boxcroft said.

Miss Pratt pressed the palms of her hands together and said, "Boxy, I hope you will assist these gentlemen from the *Examiner* with whatever information they desire."

"Mr. Boxcroft has been most helpful, Miss Pratt," Bierce said.

When Miss Pratt moved closer to me, Ted fluttered his wings. Bierce called to him, "Where's Robbie?"

"Where's Evalina?" the bird snapped back.

"Who is Evalina?" Bierce asked.

"She was my daughter," Miss Pratt said in a low voice. "She passed away a year ago. She was just two."

"Colonel Studely's daughter as well, I assume?"

"Yes," Miss Pratt said, her chin up.

"May we hope that this conversation will shortly be terminated?" Mr. Boxcroft said. "Miss Pratt and I have important business upon which to confer."

Bierce and I moved toward the March sunshine flooding into the tent. As Miss Pratt stepped along beside us, in a manner of seeing guests to the door, Ted gave a squawk, hotfooting in place.

I discovered that I had pocketed the photograph of Miss Pratt surrounded by her Praetorian guard. I halted and turned to face her. "Will you take dinner with me this evening, Miss Pratt?"

"What a pleasant prospect, Mr. Redmond! Yes, I will!" Arrangements were made before she turned back inside.

Bierce looked at me with amusement. He had accused me of having an even keener appreciation of young women than he had.

"She is a handsome and accomplished young lady, Tom," he said.

"Yes, she is!"

I did like young ladies. They were pretty, they smelled good, their voices were harmonious, their movements graceful. Their shapes implied abiding pleasures, and they eschewed the male excesses of sweating, smelling, farting, belching, hawking, spitting, and so on.

And I did like Miss Pratt.

"Eugenics," Bierce said, as though deep in thought.

CHAPTER EIGHT

ME, pro. *The objectionable case of I. The personal pronoun in English has three cases, the dominative, the objectionable and the oppressive. Each is all three.*
> — *The Devil's Dictionary*

WEDNESDAY, MARCH 16, 1892

"I am interested in them as, shall we say, suspects," Bierce said to me in his office. Behind him, out the window, the cast-iron facades of the buildings ranked away up Montgomery Street. We were discussing Dora Pratt's Praetorians, as Bierce termed them.

"Our suspects, whatever their motives, were of course aware of Bird's overweening prejudice against Studely," Bierce said. "So why not let Oz Bird take his course? What I always wonder is this: Why at all? And why now?"

"The opportunity of the parade, and Bird's threat?"

"Or an urgency of some kind?" He squinted at me. "I understand there is a certain pact among the champion women wing-shots, that their weapons will never be used against their fellow humans."

"Miss Pratt is an intelligent and honorable young woman," I said. "I have the greatest respect for her."

"She was educated as a shooter by Bird, and for the Show's forays in Europe by Studely. I quote Oliver Wendell Holmes at the breakfast table: 'A few women have had the capacity to profit from an education—Madame de Stael, for example. But a natural law is not disproved by a pickled monster.' "

"I will give her an expensive dinner this evening," I said stiffly.

"I know!" Bierce said.

Just then Mammy Pleasant entered Bierce's office, green-cloaked and with a covered basket under her arm. She wore a black straw hat with the sides of the brim fastened under her chin so that it resembled a coal scuttle encasing a dark, sharp-featured old face. She was of some age between fifty and seventy and slightly hunched. She seated herself with a bustle of movement at Bierce's behest, placing her basket beside her chair.

Mammy Pleasant cooperated with Bierce because of his favors, as she perceived them, to her race. She was an informant of both high life and low life; she had helped Negroes obtain jobs in the powerful households of San Francisco, and thus was presumed to be party to the belowstairs gossip of those establishments. It was rumored that she was very wealthy. She lived in the mansion of a prominent banker named Bell out on Octavia Street, in what capacity no one seemed to know.

Bierce said, "Mrs. Pleasant, we are concerned with a period eight years past, with a man named Isaac Guttman. As a single man living in San Francisco, he may have visited one or several of the parlor houses of this city. I wonder if you would make inquiries of women of your acquaintance who might have encountered such a person."

Mammy Pleasant said grimly, "The ladies of eight years ago are not many of them the same ladies of nowadays."

"Surely there are some."

"There's some that's madams now," Mammy nodded.

She herself was reputed to have run—not as a madam, but as the proprietor—parlor houses on Nob Hill.

She rocked a little in her chair, putting a dark, frail hand out to hold it over the chalky dome of the skull on Bierce's desk, as if to absorb some quality from it.

"I am acquainted with one or two of such, Mr. Bierce. Just what is it you want to know about this person?"

"He and Oswald Bird, of the current police alarm, were involved in the Hungry Valley shoot-out eight years ago. Bird was an exhibition shooter in a Wild West show. Nothing is known of Guttman except that the two of them entrained from San Francisco for Tulare County. After the shooting he disappeared. He may have drowned trying to escape. I would like to know if he returned to San Francisco, or if there is any knowledge of him prior to the Hungry Valley affair."

"Isaac Guttman. What would he been—rich man, poor man, beggar man, thief?" A flash of humor flickered across her face.

"I think not a rich man," Bierce said. "And perhaps not a beggar man. A gunman."

"Any description?"

"A small man. Not as aggressive as Bird; a junior partner in the Hungry Valley enterprise."

"Clean-shaven and young, I was told," I said.

Mammy slitted her eyes as though trying to recall something. "I will see what I can discover, Mr. Bierce."

She rose, gathered up her basket, slapped a hand to secure her cloak around her, and left the office. She had a peculiar style of walking, as though setting each foot precisely in front of its fellow. I felt her departure like a release of weight from my shoulders.

Bierce sighed. "I always feel a strain, with Mrs. Pleasant, of having to comport myself exactly as she thinks I will comport myself. However, I will wager that she will come up with something."

"She usually does," I said.

....

At a table by the window on the second floor of Bertrand's, in the midst of crisp white napery and gleaming flatware and glasses, mine half-filled with burgundy and Miss Pratt's a quarter empty, she and I faced each other over clear soup. Dinner at Bertrand's was a dollar and a quarter, but wine could run the bill up astronomically. I had selected a burgundy for the first courses, a chilled sauterne for the last.

My effort to obtain Miss Pratt's life story, and perhaps her favors, would cost me most of a week's salary.

She wore a gray jacket over a crisp, white, high-necked blouse and a black velvet band around her throat, a golden owl's head with jeweled eyes pinned to the band. Her hair had been neatly arranged with beau-catcher curls at the temples— perhaps for me!

"You married Oswald Bird when you were very young," I said.

"Is this why I am being feted, Mr. Redmond? So my history will be all revealed?"

"I wish it would be all revealed to Tom, if I could call you by your given name."

"Very well, Tom," she said, but she did not smile.

"I am interested not merely in your history, Dora," I said.

She sighed. "I was sixteen. We were both exhibition shooters for Texas Jack's Combination. Oz had taken me under his wing."

She stirred restlessly, as though her story had been told too many times.

"I was a girl in Missouri. My father was a drunkard and then dead, and my mother had to support three of us. I undertook to bring in game for our provender with Daddy's rifle. I became a good shot. I took part in a competition in St. Louis and won. A friend of my mother's introduced me to Texas Jack."

She sipped meagerly of her burgundy, her eyes meeting mine over the rim of her glass. I was not content to leave it at that.

"You have told me Bird was a hard taskmaster. Why did you marry him?"

"He was a hero to me, Tom."

"But he was no longer a hero after the Hungry Valley shoot-up."

"That is so."

"Oz Bird blames Colonel Studely for turning you away from him."

She shook her head once.

"But Colonel Studely undertook your education, just as Oz Bird had assisted your shooting prowess," I said. "Books? Lessons?"

"Books," she said, nodding. "I had always been a reader, when I could get books. He brought me books. He knew so much more of the world than I did—what things were important, and what were not. Worldly things. Manners. Associations! I have taken tea with Queen Victoria, and the Princess of Wales and her daughters, and the Duke of Edinburgh. I have exchanged letters with Queen Victoria! All this was due to Robbie!"

"And you bore his child, Evalina."

"Yes."

"And for some years that relation was a satisfactory one?"

She gazed at me silently. Our waiter appeared with plates of turkey and currant jelly, and Dora applied herself to the main course, no doubt pleased to think that my interrogation was over. It was not.

"That group that collected around us the other day at the Fairgrounds," I said. "Short Bear, Billy Buttons, Enrique Lopez, and I think even Darkey Duncan. They love and admire you; Bierce and I both commented on it."

She colored, and raised her chin proudly. "They are my friends," she said.

"Friends against something," I said. "Against some threat or injustice to the Ace of Shoots, against Colonel Studely, against Oz Bird."

"That is enough, Mr. Redmond!" Dora Pratt said. "If you persist in this I will leave this place!" She made a motion as though to rise from her chair. The waiter stood nearby, a napkin stretched between his hands.

"Tom," I said.

The waiter removed our plates and replaced them with slices of orange layer cake. He was making soothing sounds, aware that this meal was no longer progressing happily.

"Tom," Dora said, but she still did not smile.

"I hope to get to understand you, but I also have a murder to solve."

"Let us not solve it this evening, Tom."

"I suspect that there is some great sadness in your life," I said. "Is it the death of your Evalina? Can we speak of it?"

"No, we cannot!" Dora said forcefully. "Now stop this, please! I would like to speak of the weather now."

I sighed and said, "Do you like our San Francisco weather, Miss Pratt?"

"Dora," she said, and smiled. It was not much of a smile,
a reflexive tightening and shaping of her lips that may
have had a slight sheen of pink applied to them for this occasion, but it was the first Dora Pratt smile that had been directed at me.

"You have blessed this meal," I said.

She looked puzzled. "Why do you say that?"

"You have condescended to smile at me."

"Oh, bosh!" she said, and smiled more deeply, this time with
dimples.

THURSDAY, MARCH 17, 1892

The next morning when I looked into Bierce's office, he stood
behind his desk, facing a brown wren of a woman whom I
identified as the mysterious Miss Keith even before he introduced us.

"How do you do, Mr. Redmond? I am pleased to make
your acquaintance!" She had a small, piquant face, and her
brown hair was wrapped in an unattractive coil over one ear.
Her eyes were amazing—gray, wide, like mirrors, like windows into another dimension. I gazed into them briefly, and
then could not meet them, as though all my sins might be reflected there.

"Miss Keith has come down from her higher office to confer with the lowly inhabitants of the second floor," Bierce
said.

"In the hope of forestalling antagonisms between us,
as Mr. Bierce has been employed to attack my gender, and
I his."

Bierce said amiably, "I was not aware that I am employed to
attack your gender, Miss Keith."

"And I must caution myself not to attribute the cross purposes I have noticed at this newspaper to young Mr. Hearst's machinations," Miss Keith said.

I thought that statement must please Bierce.

"Won't you sit down, Miss Keith?" he said, and the two of them seated themselves, leaving me standing. She regarded Bierce with a pasted-on smile, her hands curled for support beneath her chin.

"So, Miss Keith, am I to understand that you are a student of machinations?"

"I am an enemy of antagonisms, Mr. Bierce."

"Surely antagonisms are warranted when another person's ideas or morals are poisonous!"

"Unnecessary, Mr. Bierce, Mr. Redmond!" she said, cutting her wonderful eyes toward me. "Antagonism never results from real, objective differences, but from a person's mixing in his own personal reactions—the extra emphasis he gives the truth, the enjoyment he takes in doing a thing because it is unpalatable to others, or the feeling that he must show his own colors. Consider Lear and Cordelia, gentlemen! What Lear thought was antagonism was surely only misunderstanding."

"What of Jesus Christ and the money changers of the temple, my good woman?"

She laughed merrily. "If Christ drove the money changers from the temple, so much the worse for Christianity!"

"And the late conflict between the states?"

"The War, also, shows the futility of antagonism. We freed the slaves by war, and now must free them all over again, individually, and pay the costs of the War and reckon with the added bitterness of Southerners besides."

She folded her arms and stated, formally, as though pledging her most personal belief: "You see, Mr. Bierce, surely we have learned that the good must be extended to all society before it can be held secure by any one person of any one class. We have not yet learned to add to that statement, that unless all men and all classes contribute to a good, we cannot be sure that it is even worth having."

Bierce said, "I believe, Miss Keith, that you are expounding to us an organized philosophy or body of thought. May we know from whence these ideas come?"

"Yes, you may, Mr. Bierce. They are the Christian and democratic policies of Miss Jane Addams, of Hull-House."

"Christian, you say! I had thought Miss Addams was a socialist."

"She is a Christian humanitarian."

"And you have been connected with Hull-House in Chicago, Miss Keith?"

"I have, sir, for my salvation."

"I see," Bierce said. He had a low opinion of Christians.

"One of these days we must hold a colloquy on the subject of the Eugenics being preached these evenings at the Mechanics' Hall, Mr. Bierce," Miss Keith said, rising.

When she had gone, I said, "She has the eyes of an angel."

Bierce leaned forward, placing his hand on the chalky dome of his desk skull. "One must remember this of angels," he said. "Christian dogma informs us that the good angels look down with pleasure and gratification upon the terrible punishment of sinners writhing in the pit below."

And he said, "I am interested in Isaac Guttman, Tom. Hat, coat, and rifle stacked on the river bank. Does that not sound as though we are meant to believe that Guttman disappeared down the river?"

"The shoot-up took place in late September," I said. "At that time of year, there would not be much water in Bosque Creek, but no one seemed able to clarify that fact when I was down there."

"The past is always difficult to clarify, Tom," Bierce said, and he asked if I would attend the lecture of Professor Franklyn with him at the Mechanics' Hall the next evening.

CHAPTER NINE

TAKE, v.t. To acquire, frequently by force but preferably by stealth.
— *The Devils' Dictionary*

FRIDAY, MARCH 18, 1892

Bierce and I presented ourselves at the Mechanics' Hall at seven o'clock that evening and paid a dollar and a half each for tickets. The hall was about a third full of earnest-looking men and women, not many of them young.

According to a sandwich board propped on the stage, Professor Franklyn was connected with the Farrar College of Moral Philosophy in New York State.

He stood at a lectern with the Stars and Stripes draped over it, a plump little fellow in a claw hammer coat, his bald head gleaming under the electric lights. Bierce slumped in his chair, glowering up at him as he lectured, an extended finger metronoming up and down as points were made.

"This great country in its second century of existence is in grave danger!" Professor Franklyn intoned, his finger jerking, "for natural selection has been replaced by what we call 'reproductive selection,' which gives the battle of our heredity to the most fertile and not the most fit."

He repeated this.

"Measures such as" (his finger counted) "the eight-hour day, advances in medicine, free clinics, and reductions in infant mortality have thus encouraged an increase in unemployables, degeneration, and feeblemindedness!

"The laws against children in factories!" Now his finger was leveled at his auditors, instead of raised vertically. "Once children were an economic asset; now they are a liability. The responsible among the working classes have, by one means or another, reduced their birth rate. The irresponsibles have not, and as we surely know, irresponsibility begets irresponsibility.

"The moral man, faithful to his wife, does not sow his seed widely. The immoral man sows widely. And the pattern spreads epilepsy, alcoholism, disability . . ."

Professor Franklyn continued this list. Bierce folded his arms on his chest.

"The immigrations from southeast Europe!" The finger rose monitorily again. "Whole families prone to burglary, drunkenness, and vagrancy! Roman Catholics and Jews, who are commanded by their religions to multiply. In a short time this nation will become darker in pigmentation, smaller in stature, and more inclined to crimes of larceny, kidnapping, assault, murder, and sexual immorality!"

There was a stirring in the audience at this dreadful news. Bierce glanced sideways at me. Professor Franklyn continued to hammer his points home with his threatening finger.

"The pauper classes are outproducing the rest of us!" he continued. He moved from behind the protection of the national banner and removed a large white handkerchief from his pocket, with which he swabbed his gleaming forehead.

He brandished his finger again. "The ratio of the feebleminded to the normal is altered every day! The immigrant laborers are now outbreeding their masters. Nothing is being done to halt our blood adulteration by blood of an inferior grade!

"What is to be done?" he cried in a louder voice.

"If superior citizens are desired, they must be bred! If inferior are not desired, they must *not* be bred. I tell you, a day must come when a woman will no more accept a man without knowing his genealogical history than would a stock breeder take a sire for his colts or calves without knowing their pedigree!"

Retreating behind the flag, he spoke more quietly. "What nature does blindly, slowly, and ruthlessly, man may now do providentially, quickly, and kindly!

"Man must take charge of his own evolution! God does not now give us stone tablets and prophecies to reveal His will. He has given man the microscope, the spectroscope, the telescope, the chemist's test tube, and the statistician's curve in order that we can produce our own revelations!"

Professor Franklyn continued in this vein, halting from time to time to dab his forehead. A few of the audience departed noiselessly, but most remained, rapt. Bierce's elbow prodded me. We took our leave of Eugenics.

"Our portrait of Colonel Studely has been fleshed out considerably," Bierce said.

"I did not like Professor Franklyn," I said.

"Yet there is a perverse rationality in his utterance."

I said, "It seems to me, a denounced Roman Catholic, that, unhappily for the race or not, the drunken unemployable still is ensured the protection of the Bill of Rights as much as is the president of Harvard."

"I would like to purchase a glass of whiskey for you in celebration of that sentiment," Bierce said.

We headed for Blessington's.

....

Over lagers, Bierce said, "You and I have been invited to a fisti-cal affair involving the Wild West Show."

"What's this?"

"You have heard of the Sam Browne–Iggy Carlinsky heavy-weight prize fight to be held aboard a grain scow up the Bay at some unspecified date?"

Indeed, all of San Francisco knew of the fight, for it was a continuing rivalry between two fighters who had each won once by a knockout. This was to be the rubber match. Because it was unlawful in California to stage fights to the finish outside of athletic clubs, the venue had to be kept a secret from the au-thorities. We knew only that it would take place aboard the barge *Commandey*. Moreover, it was a prison offense to fight without gloves, so at least some rudimentary fist-covering would be used, although most spectators would prefer bare knuckles.

"Sam Browne has broken his hand in an accident connected with his employment delivering beer barrels," Bierce said. "So the organizers had to find a replacement. They have recruited the bulldogger from the Wild West Show, who has had some success as a bare-knuckle fighter."

"Darkey Duncan!"

"You and I are invited to join Willie Hearst aboard the *Aquila* tomorrow morning, to search out the site of the combat."

SATURDAY, MARCH 19, 1892

With Ambrose Bierce, Sam Chamberlain, and yours truly aboard, the captain of the steam launch *Aquila,* young William Randolph Hearst, stood straight-backed, spread-legged, and nautical-hatted at the wheel as he scouted the Bay through patches of low fog for the anointed grain barge. Finally he fell in behind a couple of side-wheel river steamers, heavily laden with spectators, headed for the eastern shore. The barge and its tug lay a hundred yards off a rock cliff there.

The side-wheelers steamed alongside, and passengers began leaping aboard. Shouting men in derbies and shirtsleeves ranged along the rails to keep freeloaders off. Willie Hearst and his guests were treated with respect, and we found places in the growing crowd. A smooth decking of pine boards had been nailed down, and the ring posts bolted in place. More boats arrived, among them salmon fishermen in skiffs, and more men crowded in with good-natured complaints and catcalls.

Presently Iggy Carlinsky clambered aboard with his seconds and ducked into the wheelhouse to strip for the fight. He was strikingly white-skinned, with a thick torso and arms that swung out from his sides like hams. His black hair was slicked back on his head in a pompadour. He was greeted with shouts of "Jew-boy!" and, "Go it, Butcher-boy!"

"Here is our champion!" Bierce said as Darkey Duncan came aboard with his second, Billy Buttons. In a moment he had also stripped for combat—his black chest bare, a red scarf tied around his waist, and black tights on his thin legs. He looked less muscular than the butcher, but taller, and with a longer reach. Both men donned their leather gloves.

"Neither of these contenders would satisfy Professor Franklyn's criteria for proper Americans," Sam Chamberlain said. "A Jew and a Negro. I suppose he would consider it proper that they entertain us by battering each other, however."

"Who is Professor Franklyn, Sam?" Willie Hearst asked.

"He has been preaching the new social science of Eugenics at the Mechanics' Hall. It is an offshoot of Darwinism. Have you not been to hear him, Ambrose? Tom?"

"We heard his theories only last evening," Bierce said. "The blood of the nation is being contaminated by immigrants. Are we not all the descendents of immigrants?"

"Blood of the nation has a jingo sound," Willie said.

"Nor is it merely immigrants," Sam said. "It is anyone with a hereditary defect who endangers the national blood. Diseases that he claims are passed from parent to child, including drunkenness, pauperism, and feeblemindedness."

"A national pastime and two national defects then," Bierce said, to which we all laughed. He never, delivering a quip, accompanied it with a smile, but always with a stern face.

The referee, who wore a striped shirt and a derby hat, summoned the fighters to the middle of the ring.

"I will enforce the Marquis of Queensbury rules!" he told them in a brass voice. "In case of a clinch I will order you to step back one pace, which you must do or I will call a foul. Is that clear, gentlemen?"

Willie lit a cigar, squinting at the two opponents.

"Are you ready?" the referee bellowed.

The fighters' fists were raised in the approved style.

"I call time!"

"Chew his lip off, Darkey!" someone shouted.

Carlinsky leaped at the black man, bashing him so hard in the ribs that Darkey staggered. Carlinsky rushed at him again, as though to end the fight in the first round, only to encounter a right to the nose. This time Duncan crowded back and landed another right that slammed Carlinsky flat on his back, with blood all over his face.

The action continued in sanguinary mode, with Carlinsky rushing to get inside Duncan's guard and the black man holding him off with his longer reach, methodically chopping away at his opponent. Blood now spattered both men, which incited the crowd to more shouting.

At the end of the fifth round, Carlinsky sat hunched and panting in his corner, being doused with a pail of Bay water by his second. Darkey Duncan occupied his stool, high-headed and unperturbed, with Buttons leaning over to whisper to him.

It was clear that Carlinsky's wild rushes were wearing him out, but suddenly Duncan was also in trouble from a blow to the head that stunned him. The crowd shouted for the kill, polite no longer as they chose sides for "Jew-boy!" or "Nigger!" Both fighters were slipping in the blood on the planks of the ring.

Carlinsky, bleeding and exhausted, and Duncan, staggering and confused, reeled and slid, and once fell together, with the referee standing over them.

Duncan was up first, then the butcher. They staggered and whacked bloody gloves at one another. In his corner, Carlinsky was given a swig of whiskey.

In round seventeen blood streamed from his nose and mouth, bubbling with his every breath. At the end of the round he knocked Duncan down with a roundhouse to the head. The crowd was screaming, but I was sick of the whole bloody business.

So they staggered on to the twentieth round, when Duncan— in what was surely the last gasp of his strength—crowded Carlinsky against the ropes and floored him with firewood-chopping lefts and rights.

As the butcher struggled to gain his feet, his time ran out, and the fight was over.

Buttons caught up with Duncan and supported him back to his own corner, the winner. He was unenthusiasticaly cheered, as though the spectators were as exhausted as the fighters. The general exodus began.

I said to Bierce that I hoped Darkey Duncan would be excused from his bulldogging duties with the Wild West Show that afternoon.

....

He was not. At the Fairgrounds I sat in the first row of the grandstand and watched the performers passing in parade, Dora in the lead in her schoolgirl outfit, her rifle braced on her thigh. In a rank behind her were Short Bear, Billy Buttons, Enrique Garza in his huge sombrero, and Duncan, straight-backed and dignified, looking no worse for his beating. Raising a little dust, the parade passed around the grounds with cowgirls waving out the windows of the shiny Concord coach, swaying on its thoroughbraces.

The bulldogging was the fourth event. A brindle bull with an impressive set of horns trotted out of the enclosure, followed by Duncan, racing in a burst of applause after the bull on his paint pony, leaning forward with the brim of his hat blown back. He made his leap, but something went wrong. Suddenly everyone was standing. Duncan was down and the bull was up. The bull pranced over him with a flourish of horns. There was a general explosive yell.

And a shot.

The bull fell over sideways, flinging up its hooves, and Darkey Duncan rose shakily and raised a gauntleted hand in gratitude to the Ace of Shoots and her rifle.

....

When I kissed Dora Pratt in the darkness under the hood of the hack leaving the Old Poodle Dog, she laid a hand to her cheek and turned full face toward me.

"That is for your quickness on the draw this afternoon," I said.

"Is it?"

"And for the three smiles you have granted me this evening."

"All that?" Dora said, hand to cheek.

"There are more where that came from," I said.

"Your kisses taste of the wine that you have quite generously furnished this evening," Dora said.

"It is the wine that has given me the courage to attempt them," I said.

She presented her lips again, and I directed the hackie to my rooms on Sacramento Street.

CHAPTER TEN

RUM, n. *Generically, fiery liquors that produce madness in total abstainers.*
— *The Devil's Dictionary*

SATURDAY, MARCH 19, 1892

Saturday afternoon Bierce and I were commanded to Willie Hearst's office for an end-of-week celebration. On hand were Sam Chamberlain; Miss Keith; Willie's houseboy, Ah Sook; and Willie's mistress, Tessie Powers, a very pretty young woman in a flowery frock.

Willie made no attempt to conceal the fact that he kept a mistress in his mansion at Sea Point in Sausalito, across the Bay, and clearly loved to show her off. She had a cream-complexioned face fringed with clusters of fair curls. She was a very quiet, very ladylike person whom I had heard the British elite of Sausalito cut unmercifully because of her irregular position.

Chairs were provided, and Willie, tall and awkward in his navy blue suit and florid tie, directed us to them. Ah Sook poured and delivered champagne and Miss Powers offered a tray bearing a bowl of shiny black caviar in a larger bowl of ice and trimmed slices of bread.

We raised glasses in a toast to the *Examiner.* Willie then

offered a toast to me, Thomas Redmond, for my Oswald Bird efforts.

Sam was seated next to Miss Powers, who had deposited the bowl of caviar on a little table with folding legs.

"Are you a churchgoer, Miss Powers?" he asked her.

"She is a non-churchgoer who regrets that she is not a regular churchgoer," Willie said, leaning toward them in a spread-legged, proprietary stance.

"I am a small-town girl," Miss Powers said in her sweet voice. "Sunday morning services were very important when I was a young person in Winton."

Willie looked down at her with pride. Ah Sook slippered among us, tipping more champagne into raised glasses.

"Miss Keith is of the opinion that the Bible is the ancient enemy of women's progress," Bierce said, in what seemed to me a troublemaking tone. He was seated in a rather prim position, grasping his glass before him as if it were a lily.

Miss Keith smiled at him, tucking in an errant lock of hair. "It teaches that woman brought sin and death into the world, does it not?" she said.

"Does it really?" Miss Powers asked in surprise.

"The lapsarian event," Bierce said. "The fall of man as engineered by our ancestress Eve."

"Now we are in for it!" Sam said, and Willie laughed, still maintaining his supervisory posture.

"Yes, the female is held responsible for the evils that abound in this world!" Miss Keith said cheerfully. "Thus the Bible informs us that marriage, for woman, is to be a condition of bondage; she is to be dependent on man's bounty for her material wants. That is the Bible's position, and in this Christian nation the legal position as well."

I wondered if she had considered Miss Powers's illegal position as she spoke. Willie's mama—to whom the senator had left his monstrous fortune, rather than to Willie—was said to be driven to distraction by this liaison of her son's. There was much discussion at the *Examiner* of just how much longer Miss Powers would be ensconced at Sea Point, with Mrs. Hearst controlling the Hearst fortune.

"I was unaware of that in my own perusals of the Bible," Miss Powers said. "My mother had me read a chapter every Sunday before church."

"I assure you that it is there," Miss Keith said, but not insistently.

"Of course, Mr. Bierce considers marriage a bondage for men as well," Sam said.

Willie frowned, as though that were too close for comfort.

"Marriage is a condition of a master and a mistress and two slaves, making in all two," Bierce had written. *Wedlam,* he called it. *Bedlock,* he called an association such as Willie's and Miss Powers's.

"Is that so, Mr. Bierce?" Miss Keith said. "Surely you remember the difficulties of framing the Thirteenth Constitutional Amendment, which was to free the slaves from their bondage, but must not free the American female from hers? Thus the distinction: Negroes had been taken into slavery by force, but females willingly acccepted theirs at the altar!"

"I am afraid I am not a very progressive member of my gender, Miss Keith," Miss Powers said gently.

"And that is why I find you so charming, my sweet," Willie said, which seemed rather a slap at Miss Keith.

Miss Keith was not to be derailed, however. "And surely you are aware," she went on, "that clerical thunderbolts are hurled against women who take part in the suffrage movement, which they claim undermines the very foundations of society!"

"Ambrose has also written anti-clerically, you know, Miss Keith," Sam said.

"I do know!" Miss Keith said, raising her glass for Ah Sook to tip champagne into it. "He has written that heaven is a prophecy from the lips of despair, and hell only an inference from an analogy! That is very strong, Mr. Bierce!"

Bierce looked sour. He preferred to quote from his writings himself, and it was difficult for him to find himself in agreement with a feminist.

"We will hope that heaven does not have its ear turned to the *Examiner* offices!" Willie said.

"You are surely aware, madam," Bierce said to Miss Keith, "that men depend upon women to raise their morals. Consequently, it is difficult for men to surrender their immemorial notions of chastity to the suffragist free lovers."

"What a carnage of hypocrisy is thus made possible!" Miss Keith cried merrily.

The conversation soon turned to the fact that Oswald Bird had not even been seen in the City, and yet the City seemed to be besieged by him. Miss Powers was a good listener, as was Miss Keith. I thought Miss Keith an intelligent young woman, who had offended Bierce by the curious means of agreeing with his opinions about churchly matters.

Miss Keith said, "I am very sorry for Miss Pratt in what must be a misery of apprehension for her."

This was greeted with silence. Miss Keith's were the only compassionate words to be enunciated at this gathering.

....

When the celebration adjourned, Willie asked me to stay awhile, so I stood wondering what was coming my way. Miss Powers placed herself at at the window, where the late sunlight made a little halo around her neat shape.

"I have heard from our feathered friend again, Mr. Red-mond," Willie said.

For a moment I didn't know to whom he referred.

"Bird wishes another interview with you."

I cleared my throat, considering my interest in Bird's former wife.

"He has more to tell you. I recall that you pronounced your-self interested in further encounters with the fellow."

"Of course I am!" I managed to say heartily. "How do these communications come, Mr. Hearst?"

"The first was a letter. This latest came by telephone. It was a very clear connection. He has a hard voice."

Like Carborundum, as I recalled. "If he comes here, Mr. Pot-ter must be warned."

"Yes, indeed!"

"If he is not here, it would seem that he was not in the City when Colonel Studely was murdered."

Willie nodded. "That is Mr. Bierce's position, is it not?"

And he said, "Mr. Redmond, I am aware that these are dan-gerous ventures. You will be suitably rewarded."

"Thank you, Mr. Hearst."

"Bird said one more thing. He asks that you intercede with his wife."

I cleared my throat again, and asked, "Intercede how?"

"I assumed you would know what he meant."

....

Later that night, in my bed, I held Oz Bird's wife in my arms. Her lithe body with its astonishing breasts, steely forearms, and powerful passions rested there as though I were a refuge. For my part, the impatience of assisting a vibrant young woman in removing her complicated corset combined with the apprehen-sion of Oz Bird bursting through the door with a knife in one hand and a revolver in the other provided a sharpening of sensation I had never before experienced.

I told her of Willie Hearst's telephone call from Oswald Bird, and felt the ardor in her body change to shivering.

"I am to intercede with you," I said.

"I don't know what you mean!"

"It must mean to find out if you are receptive to his return."

"No!" she whispered, her breath warm against my cheek.

"I feel like John Alden with Miles Standish."

She laughed without humor.

"It sounds as though he is coming here."

She breathed against my cheek again.

I touched the rough scar on her waist.

"What's this, Dora?"

"It's just a crease."

"Gunshot?"

"Never mind it, please." She was shivering again.

"An accident?"

She sighed and said, "Yes, an accident."

"Oz?"

She would say no more about it, but she was weeping. I held her shivering body. "Tell me," I said.

"I killed a man," she said. "Oz knows. It is something I have sworn never to do—turn a firearm on a human being. Oz knows it."

"You mean he has power over you because of it?"

She pressed her wet face into my neck. "I don't know what is to become of me!"

"There are five of us to protect you," I said.

....

The morning headlines announced the murder of Arliff K. Potter:

BIRD VENGEANCE STRIKES AGAIN

....

SP EXECUTIVE MURDERED

....

MR. POTTER SHOT NEAR SP OFFICES

....

Potter had been shot in his patrolman-driven buggy when it was stopped for cross traffic at Mission Street. No one had seen the assassin.

Oswald Bird was in San Francisco.

....

I was assigned to interview other SP executives; one of them seemed oddly gratified, two of them frightened, all of them properly horrified, but none of them satisfactorily forthcoming. The railroad chief of detectives, Culver, was not available, nor was the president of the railroad, Collis P. Huntington. Nor was Mrs. Potter, in her stone-walled minor mansion on the slopes of Nob Hill. I was allowed to speak to her son, an SP employee like his father, and to her married daughter, who proffered me an obituary of her father, penned on scented notepaper. Arliff K. Potter had belonged to a great many clubs and service organizations, and to the Episcopal Church.

Everyone seemed certain that Oswald Bird would be quickly apprehended and punished.

CHAPTER ELEVEN

IMPARTIAL, adj. *Unable to perceive any promise of personal advantage from espousing either side in a controversy or adopting either of two conflicting opinions.*
— *The Devil's Dictionary*

SUNDAY, MARCH 20, 1892

In the Sunday *Examiner,* Bierce had written in "Prattle":

> *I have been asked for counsel by a friend and colleague, a journalist who is also a poet, who wishes to produce art for the purpose of reform, to lay about her slaying monsters and liberating captive maids. Unfortunately this is not "writing," this is missionary work. Literature is not a form of benevolence. It has nothing to do with "reform," and when used as a means of reform suffers accordingly and is justly unsuccessful. "Helpful" writing makes dull reading. Art will laurel no brow with a divided allegiance. The best service you can render is to write well with no care for anything but that.*

I put down the paper to answer my door. The big bull-dogger, Darkey Duncan, loomed there. I had a sudden heart-thump of consternation that this visit had to do with my night with Dora Pratt. I had been watching the window for Oz Bird, and here came this dark presence in at the door, one of her guardian watchdogs. He hulked inside. With him was the Mexican Garza, six inches shorter and with a wild, south-of-the-border mustachio. Both of them wore fancy black suiting, sparkling white shirts, and high collars; the Mexican carried his metallic-braided hat, Duncan a derby. One or both of them smelled of barbershop emollients.

On my dresser was the photograph of Dora in the midst of these and the two others.

"Senor Redmond," Garza said, with a flourish of his hand. "We come to inquire of your intentions!"

The black man's face was still swollen from the fight, and his left hand was wrapped in a bandage, his fingers protruding like burned sausages.

"How would you have them?" I said, folding my arms over my chest with a pretense of calm.

"Of the highest order, Newspape," Duncan said.

"We speak of Senorita Pratt, you understand," Garza said.

I understood.

"We must know if this attachment is genuine," Duncan said.

I indicated chairs for them, but they remained standing, shoulder to shoulder, a black-suited Dora-protection phalanx.

"Senorita Pratt has much misfortune with amor," Garza said. "We do not know her husband, you understand. But we have concern for her."

"You are her guardians," I said.

"We are her brothers," Darkey Duncan said. "Four of us."

"I saw her save your life," I said, and he nodded with a gesture of his bandaged hand to his forehead.

"Your intentions," he said.

"They are of the highest order, gentlemen," I said. "I like Miss Pratt very much. It is a great pleasure to spend time with her."

"Expensive *comida,*" Enrique Garza commented.

I wondered about the source of that information. Not Dora, surely. Were the four watching us?

"Let me tell you," Duncan said. "We have the strongest sentiments for this person's happiness. We see that she has pleasure in your company, Mr. Newspaperman. But we have come to tell you that if you serve her badly you will be served very badly." He showed me his big, dark, right fist.

I said I would not disappoint them.

"Proper hombre for proper lady," Garza said.

He made it sound like a shotgun cocked.

"You will ask," he continued, "what of us, her *hermanos?* My friend here is Negro." He raised his hands, palms flipped out in helplessness. "And I am Mexican, you think. In fact, I am *puro* Castiliano. But I have wives! I have a wife in Tehuantepec, and a wife in Guadalajara. The *jefe* is old, and an *Indio.* You ask, then, what of Beely Buttons? Well, senor, he is no-good, two-face person, but he is *hermano* also. So you see how we look to you."

"Are you heeled?" Duncan asked, folding his arms on his chest.

He meant, did I have a pistol. I did not.

They looked at each other with unreadable expressions.

"Bird didn't sound as though he intended to harm Miss Pratt," I said.

"Maybe harm you, though!" Duncan said, with a show of his underbite teeth. "He is one prize brute as far as she is concerned. But it was Rob Studely put her in that schoolgirl rig— dressed her up like a whorehouse special!"

I had not thought of that connotation of the schoolgirl dress. It was true that the fancier parlor houses supplied girls dressed as schoolgirls, as jockeys, even in military-school uniforms—for clients with special tastes.

"She could get out of it now he's dead," I said, but Garza shook his head.

Duncan did the same. "Folks pay good money to come see a schoolgirl shooting up glass balls!"

"Can she protect herself?" I asked.

"There is that swear those wingshots make," Duncan said. "Annie Oakley and the Princess Wenona, and them. Their guns will never harm a human being."

"We protect her," Garza said, thumping his chest. "We keep watch after her, you understand?"

Duncan showed me his fist again. "If Bird shows his ugly face at the Fairgrounds—"

"Happy is how we want the senorita!" Garza interrupted, and he squinted an eye at me as though aiming along a gun barrel.

And with that, they departed.

....

A messenger in a ragged sweater summoned me to Sam Chamberlain's office. Bierce had already arrived there, and he and Sam were regarding a handsome woman in black with a big hat. This was Mrs. Dierdorf from Denver. She reclined in Sam's chair in a long graceful *S,* exhibiting a fine profile. Her dress consisted of shingled tongues of black material fringed with black beads that clicked together in an intriguing manner when she changed position. She held out a languid hand to me when I was introduced.

Sam told me, "Mrs. Dierdorf entrained for San Franciso as soon as she was able."

"My poor Dilly!" Mrs. Dierdorf said.

"Dilly?" I said.

"I called him Dilly. His middle name was Dilworth, you know. An important family in Tennessee!"

She said, "Mr. Chamberlain and Mr. Bierce have been informing me of matters concerning Dilly's murder."

Bierce said to me, "Mrs. Dierdorf has, in turn, advised us that Studely was not in fact a commissioned colonel, either Confederate or Federal."

"It was an honorary title," Mrs. Dierdorf said. "He was a scout for General Sheridan." She waved a white hand, and patted it to her yawn. "So fatiguing, the railroad cars!" she said. "Delay after delay."

Bierce had written that passengers on the SP Railroad were subjected to the dangers of senility.

"My poor golden boy!" Mrs. Dierdorf said, in the voice of fatigue rather than that of acute sorrow.

"A man difficult to know, for us who are investigating his murder," Bierce said.

"A dear man," Mrs. Dierdorf said. "To me, not to all!" A smile wisped over her pouty mouth. "A man set in his ways, a man who commanded admiration, if not affection. A man who demanded perfection!" The smile again. "He called me his perfect one!"

The perfect one did not seem consumed by grief for her golden boy.

"And will you be staying in San Francisco awhile, Mrs. Dierdorf?" Sam wanted to know.

"A beautiful city," Mrs. Dierdorf said. "Denver is so . . . *Denver!* We will see, Mr. Chamberlain."

"Your late husband, Mr. Alfred Dierdorf, was a man of some renown in mining circles," Bierce said.

"Yes, Alfred was a man of renown!" Mrs. Dierdorf continued. "I have known many such men in my life. My golden boy was one of the most illustrious! I do love to pay regard to an illustrious man. Men such as yourselves, Mr. Bierce, Mr. Chamberlain! And I do see that Dilly's Professor Franklyn is presently lecturing in San Francisco."

"His subject Eugenics," Bierce said.

"Dilly *did* admire that peculiar gentleman! Attended his lectures in Denver."

"Mrs. Dierdorf, will you tell us exactly why you have come to San Francisco at this time?" Sam said.

She breathed a long sigh. "Because I hoped you gentlemen would inform me of the facts of this dreadful business. And now I understand Oswald Bird has murdered again! Tell me, what is being done to apprehend this creature?"

"He is being sought by law officers statewide," Sam said.

"Surely there is another reason for your presence here, Mrs. Dierdorf," Bierce said.

Her beads clicked as she moved a little to face him more directly. "Dilly owed me a sum of money, for which I am sure Mr. Boxcroft will take responsibility. And I must see Boxy on other matters, also."

"And Miss Pratt?" I said.

Her dark eye flicked at me. "I have nothing to say to Miss Pratt, Mr. Redmond!"

"I wonder if you would mind telling us how much money is involved," Sam said.

Mrs. Dierdorf smiled at him. "That is my own particular business, Mr. Chamberlain."

"We have been wondering," Bierce said, "who among the

personnel of the Show might have had motive for the murder of Colonel Studely."

"Miss Pratt has already been mentioned," Mrs. Dierdorf said swiftly.

"And what motive would that be?"

"One of the most common, Mr. Bierce."

"A woman spurned, you mean?"

"If you will put it so. And, of course, dear Boxy. My late husband's wisdom was that you could never be too suspicious of the men who have access to your money."

"Yes, that is wise, Mrs. Dierdorf," Sam said.

"And who knows who else? My golden boy could be very hard on those he found in dereliction of their duties."

"Anyone in particular, madam?" Bierce said.

"Ah, I can only think of no one and everyone, just now," Mrs. Dierdorf said, patting her lips again. She moved a shoulder in her fatigue, with another clicking of beads.

"I do recall that there was a terrible quarrel over an animal belonging to one of the performers," she went on. "Dilly simply put his foot down about having the smelly cur on the premises! There were hard feelings, I believe."

The interview was concluded by Bierce and Sam Chamberlain, between whom a competition for Mrs. Dierdorf's favor seemed to have arisen. They carried her off to the Palace Hotel for lunch while I took myself home to change my clothes before attending the Sunday afternoon show at the Fairgrounds.

I had a feeling like a hard finger poked into my back that my second meeting with Oz Bird was going to occur sooner rather than later.

CHAPTER TWELVE

FORGETFULNESS, n. A gift of God bestowed upon debtors in compensation for their destitution of conscience.
— *The Devil's Dictionary*

SUNDAY, MARCH 20, 1892

When I opened the street door to my rooms, a man in a black hat sat in the chair at the typewriter table, my bottle of brandy on the table before him, a glass in his hand. A black revolver was balanced on top of the typewriter. Oz Bird grinned at me.

I didn't have to consider how he got in, I kept a spare key behind a broken brick beside the door, which would be the first place any burglar would look. Bird raised the glass in a kind of salute. His whiskers were longer, but not a beard yet. He wore a blue miner's shirt, and a bandana loosely knotted at his neck. I had an inclination to cross myself.

"Hullo, Redmond," he said.

"I heard from Mr. Hearst you wanted to see me."

"That's right."

"Every policeman in the City must be looking for you."

"Policeman catches sight of me, he will plain curl up and faint of fright." He said this in a harsh but friendly tone. He tipped a little more brandy into his glass.

Trying to straighten out my thoughts, I said I was just back from Tulare County, where I'd been trying to find out what happened there eight years ago.

Bird grunted. "Blew four sandlappers to hell, that's what happened there! Come foggin' and fannin' at me like crazy men!"

"With some help from your pal Guttman."

"About as much help as a limp dick! Took one shot at a farmer come galloping at us out of the cornfield there and then run like a rabbit. *I* picked 'em off!" His eye squinting, finger pointing, thumb snapped like the hammer of a revolver, he said, "One, two, three, *four!*"

He regarded me with a thin-lipped smile.

"Proposition for you," he said. "I have chose you to tell my life history in print!"

"What?" I said. *What?*

"My daddy, me, my wife—all shooters. My daddy was a gunslinger for the vigilantes here, my wife the Ace of Shoots! And me! Understand you come from up Sacramento way. My people farmed just over the line in Placer County up there."

I understood that Bird hankered to see more of himself in print.

I sidled past him to drop into my easy chair. "Miss Pratt no longer considers herself your wife," I said.

"She swore to it. I don't give no mind to a bunch of papers. Robbie Studely kissed her neck and told her he'd make an eddicated woman out of her, and got her in bed and signing papers. She's coming away with Oz Bird! You tell her that for me!"

"Intercede for you."

"What's that?"

"Mr. Hearst said you wanted me to intercede with her."

"You be careful of her, hear? She has got a way of sucking a person right into carrying her kit-bag."

I knew that.

"Here's something for the newspaper," he said, pointing a finger. "I didn't shoot Robbie Studely. I was in Sacramento on the thirteenth and I can prove it! You write that for Mr. Hearst!"

"What about Potter?"

He squinted at me. "Ought to be some smart money, you writing about me, wouldn't you say?"

"I couldn't say."

He cocked his head. "Tell you what you are thinking. You will play along with Oz Bird and first chance you get you will turn him in to the law." He tapped the revolver where it rested on top of the typewriter. "You will not do that, understand?"

I nodded that I understood.

"You going to do this with me, Redmond?"

"I suspect I don't have a choice."

"Make some money for me and Dory to set up on! Tell her I'll have tickets for San Diego, and across to Tijuana and gone.

"Now listen: All these shooters will tell you how they learned to shoot because they had to support their starving fambly picking off squirrels, or some such. Frank Butler and Annie. Dora, too. Not me. I practiced shooting cats."

"Cats?" I said.

"You gonna take notes, Redmond?"

"There's a notebook in the drawer there."

He tossed me the notebook and a pencil, and took another swig of brandy, his Adam's apple at work. "Cats!" he said. "There was an old biddy lived near by us there that must've had her two hundred cats. You never saw so many cats! And there was a kind of shed outside my upstairs window there, that they'd get up on nights and yowl and squawl around. I took to picking them off with my daddy's handgun. One yowl, dead cat!" He made the gesture again, eye squinted, finger pointed, thumb snapping like the hammer of a revolver. "Then I started going out with a rifle, shooting cats. I cleared them cats out! And rabbits!" He chuckled. "You got that, Redmond?"

I had enough of that.

Next there was a long story about his first meeting with Texas Jack and how he impressed Texas Jack by shooting at empty fruit cans lined up on top of a fence. He had come to Dora Pratt's arrival in Texas Jack's Combination when he said, "That's enough for now. You get this in the paper, Redmond. I didn't shoot Robbie Studely, hear?"

He rose, pocketing the revolver, and froze, gazing at the photograph of Dora and her *hermanos* propped against the mirror on the dresser. He stepped over to snatch it up for a closer look.

"Who's that with her?"

"Her guardians."

"Guardians for what?

"Against you."

He held the photograph closer. "There's Billy! Who's them others?"

He listened, squinting, as I named them. He pocketed the photograph and was gone. I was finally able to uncross my fingers.

....

At the Fairgrounds all was preparation for the afternoon show: dust in the air, the healthy reek of manure, horses crisscrossing the field. I spotted Darkey Duncan, leaning low across his pony's neck as he chased across the middle distance. Dora had retired to her tent, where she sat in solitude before her shooting performances. I moved on along the grounds to where Short Bear was practicing knife throws.

A human shape had been chalked on a wooden wall, and the

Ponca Chief stood gazing at it, knife in hand, the black hafts of three more protruding above his belt. He was a square-built man, not tall, with a plump waistline in his soiled deerskin shirt, jeans trousers, and moccasins. His graying hair was held back with a thong.

His dark face jerked toward me as I approached, and a queer maneuver manipulated his barracuda jaw, squinted his eyes, and eroded his face in wrinkles. Short Bear was grinning a welcome.

He made a saluting gesture. In his breast pocket was a sheaf of the postcards like those I had seen in Studely's tent, which he sold to his admirers. He extracted one and presented it to me. Depicted was a younger, slimmer chieftain in full hundred-feather headdress, standing with great dignity in his fringed buckskin suit.

"For you, young white eye!" he said in what was meant to be a pleasant tone.

"Thank you, Chief Short Bear!"

He made a gesture of welcome to his space.

"You come Missy Aceyshoot?"

I had.

"You like Missy Aceyshoot?" he said, nodding vigorously.

Another pledge of allegiance was called for.

I told him I had had a visit from Oz Bird, who still considered Dora his wife.

Short Bear sucked in his lips, dissolving the savage grin, and made a motion as though to fling the knife. "Bad man!" he growled.

Garza galloped up and slid off his pony all in one elegant motion. He wore a checked shirt, gauntlets, and his big hat. "Senor Redmon'!"

Billy Buttons, mounted, was also approaching.

"Come to the Jacal, we must speak there!" Garza said.

Darkey Duncan joined us in the Jacal, where milk and coffee heated in twin pots on an iron grill over coals. We sat on benches at a scrubbed wood table, imbibing sweet, pale coffee from thick mugs; Dora's four protectors loomed at one end, and I was seated at the other.

I told of my visit from Oz Bird. "He intends to take her away with him. He said to San Diego and across the border there."

Short Bear grunted contemptuously.

Duncan started to speak, but swung around instead. Fifty feet away, Dora was in sight. She stood atop a trotting paint pony in her schoolgirl dress, rifle to her cheek, firing at glass balls a cowhand tossed up for her. Her skirt was wind-plastered against her stockinged legs.

"I wish she'd get out of that silly dress," I said.

The guardians looked at me with their various expressions, some friendly, some critical of my statement.

"Back in Oz's time she just wore a buckskin skirt and a regular shirt," Billy Buttons said.

He made gestures, outlining a proper costume. He had an off-center nose and a black bar of mustache that somehow did not pull his other features together.

"Bird doesn't consider her divorced," I said.

"We'll divorce him!" Duncan said, his bull-biting jaw set. "We trust on you, Newspape," he said. He did not say it in a friendly tone.

They all regarded me grimly. Short Bear produced a little corncob pipe with a short stem, which he loaded and lit. He blew smoke, scowling through it. He tapped his shirt, where the tops of the store of postcards protruded.

"Mr. Robbie!" he said contemptuously.

"Told Short Bear he had to give him half of what he sells

those photographs for," Duncan said. "Couldn't stand any money getting away from him. Couldn't stand being wrong about anything. Had to be right! Somebody else had to done whatever it was went wrong. Always somebody else's fault. Perfect Robbie Studely!

"It was the poor people that was ruining the country, he said. Went on about it. You can bet it was knee-grows that never asked to come over here! Immi*grunts!*"

"Feebleminded ought to be shot," Duncan went on. "Paupers ought to starve. He would go on about it, blaming, blaming. Couldn't stand anything that was broke or scarred up. Somebody had to be blamed. You see Miss Dory out there practicing. *She* had to be perfect!"

"There was a dispute over a dog," I said. A dozen horses trotted by, heading for the barn, a cowboy whooping them along.

Glances fixed on Billy.

"I had this ol' dog," he said. "There was a fuss about him between Robbie and Miss Dory."

"One day she had her own tent set up," Duncan said. "Everybody knew it was over."

"Mean to her then," Garza said, his sombrero nodding.

"That's when Robbie turned mean on her," Billy agreed, nodding. "Spiel about how much better than her Annie Oakley was, how he'd had to teach her manners and proper grammar. How she'd been brought up a country clodhopper and had no manners and was ignorant, and he had to professor her along before he could take her before the crowned heads of Europe. Like that."

"Too bad she'd take such *stuff* off him!" Duncan said. He rose, big-chested, and stood frowning down at me. The others drifted away. The parade that preceded the show would begin soon.

"Don't you fret Oz Bird," Duncan said to me. "We will clean his slate for him, don't you worry about that. Hear?"

I heard.

I went back to town to write of my visit from the outlaw, who claimed he had not shot Colonel Studely.

CHAPTER THIRTEEN

LUMINARY, n. *One who throws light upon a subject; as an editor by not writing about it.*

— *The Devil's Dictionary*

SUNDAY, MARCH 20, 1892

In "Prattle," Bierce had written:

> *These new Darwinians contend that biology is destiny and genetics the law of life, and that all deleterious traits of the human race stem from heredity. The most strict of these fellows would sterilize or castrate every man or woman who smokes, drinks a glass of beer, indulges in illicit sexual relations, or dares to doubt the literal veracity of the Bible. The punishment for murder, of course, would be the hanging of the murderer's grandfather.*

MONDAY, MARCH 21, 1892

In the morning Bierce informed me that he had heard from Mammy Pleasant.

"The proprietor of the boardinghouse on Second Street remembers Isaac Guttman," he said. "She claims to have been questioned by various sheriffs and detectives eight years ago. She doesn't know what happened to him."

"Mrs. Pleasant is pursuing the matter?"

"She is. Come, we are due for a session with the higher office."

Upstairs, the proprietor of the *Examiner* greeted us with his usual politeness. Out his windows the buildings on Montgomery Street were hazed in an aqueous atmosphere. There was a flutter of pigeon wings on the ledge. Sam Chamberlain joined us.

"The City is an armed camp, fearful of Mr. Bird," Willie said. "And he has had the temerity to call on you, Mr. Redmond!" He held up the pages of my piece.

"Tom has also become Miss Pratt's confidante," Bierce said.

Sam and Willie gazed at me as though a new aspect of my character had been revealed. I felt myself a false confidante.

"Does that mean," Sam said thoughtfully, "that Oz Bird may find reason to consider you in the same light as he considered Colonel Studely?"

"Yes, it may," I said.

Now the gaze of Willie and Sam Chamberlain became that of *Examiner* newspapermen interested in a gee-whiz event.

"I can't believe," Willie said slowly, "that the police, the sheriffs of this state, and the Southern Pacific Railroad's own detectives will not soon render Mr. Bird harmless."

"I hope you're right," I said.

....

"You say that Miss Pratt is a woman of sorrows." Bierce said to me when we had returned to his office.

"Certainly there has been tragedy in her life."

"Her child, Evalina, whom she mentioned. What do you know of that?"

"Died at the age of two, as you also heard. It is all I know. Of course, there was her marriage, and her bedlock with Studely."

"The past is the realm of sorrows," Bierce said, quoting himself. "Tom, the Hungry Valley shootings are very relevant to this matter."

"Gizzard," I said.

"I believe Gizzard was not Guttman," Bierce said.

At the Fairgrounds I found Dora in her schoolgirl dress in the Jacal having tea with none other than Miss Keith.

"I intend to write a column on Miss Pratt," the feminist journalist said to me. "She is a great credit to our gender."

I seated myself at Dora's invitation. Under her schoolgirl hat, she looked pleased at the attention. Her dimples appeared as she smiled at Miss Keith.

"She says I am a jewel of my sex!" she said to me.

"It seems that women are better exhibition shootists than men," I said.

"Why is that, I wonder?" Miss Keith said. "Is it some quietness of demeanor or spirit? Some passivity or steadiness that men, in their more virile occupations, do not possess?"

I confessed that I was stumped.

"Of course, women have been good at many things, when they were permitted," Miss Keith went on. "In Mary Magdalene we have a figure in Our Lord's story who was not a disciple only because of anti-feminism among the other disciples." She smiled a tight smile at me. "And in Miss Pratt, we have one of the best rifle shots in the world!"

"You see this childish dress I wear?" Dora said. "It was dictated by Colonel Studely. I protested, to no avail!"

Miss Keith laughed at this. It occurred to me to warn her against showing any of her poetry to Bierce.

I found myself a little miffed that she and Dora got along so well. To assert my own position, I reminded Dora that we were to have dinner together.

My hackie turned in in front of the Cyrus Hotel. The lights from the windows were streaked with the veils of rain. A doorman stood under the canopy to the street, on the gleaming sidewalk. As I struggled with my umbrella, Dora, who must have been watching through the window, came outside under the canopy and stood there a moment with the doorman. I halted in shock, seeing her, my umbrella half-raised. In her flat black hat and her black duster, her small figure looked exactly as Jake Burchard had described Isaac Guttman. "I think Gizzard was not Guttman," Bierce had said.

....

"What is it that has come between us?" Dora whispered over dinner at Malvolio's, holding up her wineglass as though to fend something off.

"Please let us enjoy ourselves," I said. "We will discuss the matter later."

"Is it Miss Keith?"

"It is not Miss Keith."

But a discussion of Miss Keith followed.

"She is a feminist," I said. "What Bierce would call a 'henarchist.' "

"She has had unhappy relations with your gender," Dora said, pushing her pasta with her fork. "You must be aware that that has been the experience of many women."

"Of you, for instance," I said. "Oz Bird and Colonel Studely."

She looked down at her plate, her small chin set. "They were the men who entered my life. I think that is the case with most women."

....

After dinner, in a hack on the way to Sacramento Street, I said, "I believe we are being observed. I hope it is not Oz Bird."

"I think it is not," she murmured.

"Is it one of your guardians?"

"Watching out for Oz."

In my rooms I helped her off with her damp duster and hung it behind the door. She sat on the edge of the easy chair, regarding me with a stiff face.

"It appears that Ike Guttman was not Ike Guttman," I said, and something rose in my throat to choke me when I saw the sadness suffuse her face. She gazed at me steadily, and she nodded.

"Will you sit down so you are not standing over me like an interrogating policeman?"

I sat down, facing her.

"My husband's partner had abandoned him in what I was told would be a very profitable cooperation with the railroad. Oz had an idea we might retire from the Show to farming, so I must help him. We would be required to display rifles, but no violence was anticipated. We would be in a righteous case because he was to be deputized."

"Who began the shooting?"

She looked down. "I don't know. Either Oz shot at the leader-fellow, or he shot at Oz."

"And your part?"

"I didn't want to shoot anybody! But a farmer came galloping out of the cornfield on a big white horse. He shot me!" She laid a hand to her side. "I shot back!"

"How did you escape?" I asked.

"I wore a dress under my duster, and I made a kind of bonnet out of a scarf. I found a maiden lady rocking on her veranda, and I said I had come to call on a man named Brewer—that was the farm Oz had optioned—but there was gunfire in that direction, which frightened me. She had her handyman take me to the railroad depot in Custis in the trap."

"Oz can reveal that you were Guttman and killed a farmer. I suppose you would go to prison."

She had removed her broad hat, and she laid her hands to the sides of her head.

"Bird told me he had only to snap his fingers and you would come back to him. Is that what he means by the snap of his fingers?"

She gazed into my eyes. "He knows I killed a man."

"And you divorced him because he had tricked you."

"Because he was a murderer who had tricked me into becoming a murderer! Because he was a brutal, hateful man!"

"What part did Studely play in this?

"He was . . . kind. He courted me. After Oz, I thought he was a good man. He was my professor. He brought me into the company of royalty. I have conversed with two queens, Tom!"

Her eyes gleamed with tears as she gazed at me.

"I have good news for you," I said. "Oz Bird told me that Ike Guttman was no use to him, that he killed four men himself. He has told me that twice now."

She covered her face with her hands, shaking her head.

"I believed him."

"He was boasting."

"I didn't think so."

"I do not miss very often, Tom."

"I think you missed when you shot at a person."

She had stopped shaking her head.

"In any case," I went on, "I will swear, and it is true, that he told me he shot four men in Hungry Valley."

"Thank you," she whispered.

TUESDAY, MARCH 22, 1892

The next morning the headlines read

BIRD: I DID NOT SHOOT STUDELY!

AN INTERVIEW WITH A TRAINROBBER

BIRD AS A CAT MARKSMAN

CHAPTER FOURTEEN

EVANGELIST, n. *A bearer of good tidings, particularly (in a religious sense) such as assure us of our own salvation and the damnation of our neighbors.*

— *The Devil's Dictionary*

TUESDAY, MARCH 22, 1892

A detective came to the *Examiner* to escort me to a meeting with Chief O'Brien at Old City Hall.

"Now, just why did Oz Bird come to call, Redmond?" O'Brien wanted to know, leaning over his desk toward me.

"He wants me to write his history."

"That was what he took the chance of coming to see you for?"

"So he said."

"When're you going to do this with him?"

"Some of his youth he described. No arrangement was made for another interview."

"Why didn't you report this, Redmond?"

"A .44 revolver was prominently displayed."

"You suppose he's in touch with Miss Pratt?"

"I'm sure not," I said.

"Something don't sound just right to me," Chief O'Brien said.

WEDNESDAY, MARCH 23, 1892

With Bierce was a skinny young man with a crust of blond beard. He was tapping a finger on the cranium of Bierce's desk skull. He glanced back at me with a grin when I entered the office.

He was Marshall McGee's assistant, Jake Burgess. McGee was the *Chronicle*'s bad copy of Bierce, his "Ponyfeathers" a bad copy of "Prattle." The *Chronicle* and the *Examiner* were engaged in a circulation war, and the *Examiner* employed many of the circulation-raising devices Willie Hearst had learned from Joseph Pulitzer's *Journal* before coming to California to beg the *Examiner* from his father, Senator Hearst. The *Examiner* had led the way with baseball scores, song lyrics, and murder investigations on the front page, and employed journalists such as Bierce and me as detectives.

McGee and Burgess, whom I viewed as reflections in a distorted mirror of Bierce and myself, must also be investigating the murder of Colonel Studely.

Jake Burgess said, "I see Oz Bird leaves his calling card from time to time, Tom."

Bierce said, "Mr. McGee and Mr. Burgess are investigating the murder of Arliff K. Potter."

"Asking me to believe you fellows are not?" Burgess said, blinking his eyes in ironic disbelief.

"Not," I said, feeling thrown out at first. Bierce was wearing his impenetrable expression.

Burgess dug a coin from his pocket, flipped it once so we could see that it was gold, and slapped it down on the desk. It was a medal, not a coin, with a figure of the goddess of Justice, scales in hand, on one side. When Burgess turned the coin over, revealed was a sideways V enclosing a circle—an open eye.

"Know what this is?" Jake asked.

I didn't.

"It has to do with vigilance," Bierce said.

Burgess nodded, grinning. "These medals were struck for the Second Vigilance Committee when it broke up in 1857."

"And this belonged to Mr. Potter?" Bierce said.

"Keerect!"

"May I inquire how you came into its possession?"

"Mrs. Potter," Burgess said, and rolled his eyes.

Bierce leaned back in his chair with his fingers tipped together. "Let me recall. The Second Vigilance Committee was convened on the subject of voting irregularities and a couple of murders. Casey and Cora were hanged, Cora after he made an honest woman of Belle Ryan. Two or three others were also hanged. A number of criminals were exiled; others fled."

Burgess made a clapping motion. "Fellow named Borland was shot last week up by Roseville, persons unknown. Borland was an older fellow."

"Second Vigilance Committee?" I asked.

"Keerect."

"You are thinking that some relative of Casey or Cora is looking for vengeance?"

"Wondering if you might be thinking that."

"We were not, I can assure you," Bierce said.

"The *Chronicle* brings you the latest news," Burgess said, rising.

"Good luck with it," Bierce said. "And my regards to Mr. McGee."

Burgess saluted and sauntered lankily out.

Bierce bared his teeth at me.

I said, "So they are thinking that Bird shot Studely, but not Potter, while we are thinking the opposite."

"I believe Mr. Burgess was just fishing," Bierce said.

"Should I look into Mrs. Potter, and this Borland?"

Bierce made a fist and raised it, but then let it down gently. He nodded. "Even though I believe this particular matter has no validity."

THURSDAY, MARCH 24, 1892

Research in the files of the *Call* and the *Chronicle* recovered some events of 1856:

Charles Cora shot U.S. Marshal William Richardson in a quarrel over an exchange of insults to Richardson's wife and to Cora's mistress, the flamboyant madam Arabella Ryan. James Casey ambushed and shot dead the crusading editor James King. Both—Casey and Cora—were in the city jail when the Vigilance Committee, reconstituted from 1851, extracted them from the jail and hanged them. Two other murderers, Philander Brace and Joseph Hetherington, on whom I found no specific information, were also hanged. Peter Wightman and the corrupt Judge Edward Walton were sought, but escaped the City. A number of others were deported to Australia: Billy Mulligan, Yankee Sullivan, and Martin Gallagher as "disturbers of the peace of our city, destroyers of the purity of our elections, active members of organized gangs who have invaded the sancity of our ballot-boxes"; Billy Carr, Mike Brannigan, and William McLean were also deported for ballot-box offenses; and some twenty others on other charges. Many petty criminals, feeling threatened, also left town.

A year or so later the Committee repealed its sentences of exile, and many of the deportees returned. Several brought lawsuits—most for damages but some on criminal charges— against individual Vigilance Committee members. These suits were unsuccessful but involved a good deal of nuisance. There were also some physical attacks.

There were simply too many names, offenses, and possibilities to be dealt with by a couple of journalists.

....

That afternoon Bierce and I again met with Willie Hearst and Sam Chamberlain in Willie's big corner office.

Bierce said, "Tom and I have been looking into the murder of Colonel Studely as having been accomplished by someone else in the hope that Oswald Bird, who threatened his life, would be blamed for the crime. There is, however, the possibility that the attendant murder of Arliff Potter was similarly committed— one or the other, or both, with Bird to take the blame."

Willie raised his eyebrows. No doubt he was disappointed by the lack of progress in the Studely case, but he knew better than to announce that fact to Bierce.

Bierce said, "I must tell you that as Tom and I have been investigating the murder of Colonel Studely, Marshall McGee and Jacob Burgess of the *Chronicle* have been investigating that of Potter."

Willie leaned back in his chair. Sam sat beside the desk, a gardenia in his buttonhole. Sam leaned forward, grinning. He did appreciate any obstacles that Bierce encountered.

"We feel that the Studely suspects are limited to five," Bierce went on. "In the Potter case, if Mrs. Potter is to be believed, the suspects have no such limitations, in number or in time."

"What do you mean by that, Mr. Bierce?" Willie wanted to know.

Bierce explained the connection with the Second Vigilance Committee of thirty-six years ago.

"Oh, my goodness!" Sam said.

"I believe that must be looked into, also," Bierce said. "If you wish us to continue, Mr. Hearst."

"Of course I want you to continue!" Willie said. "Nor is there any pressure to finish this up—is there, Mr. Chamberlain?"

"Certainly not!" Sam said.

But of course there was, and no doubt the two of them had been discussing it.

"I will tell you what you might look into," Sam said. "I have met a Miss Opal Merkle, a very charming young actress in *Our American Cousin*, currently playing at the Eagle Theater. Miss Merkle informed me that she is the granddaughter of a Judge Walton, who was persecuted by the Vigilance Committee."

Miss Merkle had been given a certain amount of attention in the newspapers, perhaps more for her personal charms than for her thespian talents.

Bierce would be interested in a charming young actress.

"It shall be looked into," he said.

....

The Potter mansion was a tall, narrow structure on the western slope of Nob Hill. Mrs. Potter, a slow-moving older lady in black with a powerful bosom and a kind of black napkin settled over her hair, its point on her forehead. Her son, William Potter, whom I had met before, was with her. We were invited into the gloomy parlor, where Mrs. Potter occupied the chair of honor and her son stood at her side.

Bierce expressed himself on the subject of her husband's murder. I said that I had seen him in his office only ten days before. Bierce confessed that we had heard of the Vigilance Committee connection from Mr. Jacob Burgess of the *Chronicle*.

"A very polite young man," Mrs. Potter said, settling her shoulders in a way that made me think we had uphill work before us.

"Indeed, madam," Bierce said. "We had assumed the outlaw Oswald Bird to be the perpetrator of the tragedy, until Mr. Burgess described your own suspicions."

"Oswald Bird *was* the assassin!" young William Potter announced.

"My son thinks he was," Mrs. Potter said. "I do not."

"Your husband was a member of the Vigilance Committee?"

"He believed powerfully in the good the Committee accomplished," she said, nodding.

"Including the hanging of four murderers," Bierce said. "Is it from the descendants of one of these that you think an act of vengeance has taken place?"

As her son spoke again, Mrs. Potter settled herself once more with her arms folded over her bosom and her lips sucked in disagreeably.

"My father told me he was very worried about Bird," he said. "He took steps to protect himself from Bird, Bird was always on his mind after that interview in the *Examiner!*"

"Which was written by my associate," Bierce said.

William Potter frowned at me.

Mrs. Potter said, "It is also true that my husband was fearful all his life because of events that took place after the Vigilance Committee was dissolved."

"What events would those have been, Mrs. Potter?"

"There were letters, threats. There was an encounter of some kind. Mr. Potter was a secretive man, Mr. Bierce. He did not confide in me."

"You do not have the letters?"

"I have searched for them. I am sure he destroyed them."

William moved a foot forward to separate himself from his mother's chair.

"He was not secretive about Oz Bird," he said.

"Bird certainly felt he had been wronged by your father, and by the Railroad," I said.

William said forcefully, "The railroad was being unfairly criticized over the Hungry Valley affair, and my father proceeded as he was instructed."

"So he understood Bird's anger."

"Yes, he did!"

"But there was something in his past that affected him, madam?" Bierce said.

"Mr. Potter honored the Vigilance Committee," she said firmly. "My son says that Mr. Potter had regrets about the treatment of Mr. Bird. But I assure you that he had none about the treatment of the felons of San Francisco by the Vigilance Committee!"

She rocked a little in her chair, her arms still clasped to her bosom. "There was a person," she said. "I saw him once. Mr. Potter pointed him out to me on Sutter Street. Mr. Potter said that it was unfortunate, sometimes, the men one had to employ. I suppose that meant this person was in the employ of the Vigilance Committee. He was a skinny little man, dressed all in black, with a white face. I thought he looked like death."

There was a silence of some weight.

"Was there a name attached, madam?" Bierce asked.

She shook her head. "It was an ugly name that seemed to me fitting."

A silence of more weight. Guttman.

CHAPTER FIFTEEN

SIREN, n. One of several musical prodigies famous for a vain attempt to dissuade Odysseus from a life on the ocean wave. Figuratively, any lady of splendid promise, dissembled purpose and disappointing performance.

— *The Devils' Dictionary*

FRIDAY, MARCH 25, 1892

There was a young beauty in Bierce's office when I turned in, a slim figure in a blue gown with a matching umbrella and surely ten pounds of the milliner's art shading her features. Bierce stood facing her.

"May I introduce my colleague, Mr. Redmond?" he said.

Her bright face swung toward me, pink lips exposing white teeth, green eyes, a pert jut of nose. A charming bosom was suggested.

She was posed in the chair facing Bierce's desk, one hand flattened over the chalky dome of Bierce's desk skull, not quite touching it.

"Miss Merkle is having a fine success in *Our American Cousin,*" Bierce told me.

"A full house all this week!"

"Congratulations, my dear!"

The best of men became foolish confronted by the wiles of pretty young women.

Bierce made a gesture indicating that I should stay.

I said I had yet to see *Our American Cousin,* but had heard many compliments.

"Thank you, Mr. Redmond!"

"I did think your young man in the play was a trifle skittish," Bierce said.

"We will see that that is corrected, Mr. Bierce. Mr. Perkin will be skittish no longer!"

"The skittishness was, of course, understandable in your presence, Miss Merkle," Bierce said.

I muttered to myself.

Bierce had seated himself, and appeared at ease. The subject turned to Miss Merkle's childhood.

"No, I did not have a happy childhood, Mr. Bierce. Did you?"

"I was not a happy young person in the War Between the States," Bierce said.

He gave me an embarrassed smile. "And were you a happy young person in Sacramento, Tom?"

"Very happy," I said.

"The simple delights of childhood," Bierce said. "Your grandfather was Judge Walton, Miss Merkle?"

"Yes, he was." She straightened, tucking in her chin, and gazed hard at him.

"Miss Merkle, Mr. Redmond and I are concerned with a matter involving the Second Vigilance Committee. We understand that your grandfather had some experience with it."

"Indeed he did!" All at once she seemed a very different

person, high-headed and intense, with color in her cheeks. "My grandfather was accused by the Vigilance Committee of selling his judicial decisions to the criminal element. He was tried in absentia and found guilty, but by that time had fled the state. He might have returned after the Committee disbanded, but he was disposed against California and chose to remain in Chicago, where he had resumed his career as an attorney."

"And you feel he was ill-treated by the Committee?"

"Indeed I do, Mr. Bierce! The Vigilance Committee did not consist of disinterested men, you know."

"Tell me, Miss Merkle," Bierce said.

"Who were these persons who presumed to judge their fellow men? It has been suggested by others than myself that many of them were no better than those they chose to hang or to exile. Those who were not villains may have been merely failures, disgusted with a lack of proper law enforcement, anxious for some kind of control over the destiny that had denied them—all those attitudes of men to whom the place to which they have devoted themselves has been a disappointment, and who by their own choices happened to be inside Fort Gunnybags rather than outside!"

She spoke her lines with fervor. I found myself impressed. I knew of Fort Gunnybags as the Geary Street headquarters of the Vigilance Committee, which had been fortified by walls of stacked-up sandbags.

"My grandfather suffered a great injustice, Mr. Bierce," Miss Merkle continued. "He had presided at a trial where the gambler Charles Cora was not convicted of the murder of U.S. Marshal Richardson. There was a hung jury because there was considerable evidence that the marshal had been the aggressor in the shooting. Two men were accused of having been bribed by Cora's paramour; they were taken into custody by the Committee. My grandfather's arrest was also sought. I am not in favor of vigilante justice, Mr. Bierce!"

"As you know, the Committee is usually honored in San Francisco."

She slumped a little. "It was responsible for my unhappy childhood in Chicago. And for my family's misery."

"I understand."

She straightened again, and spoke in her fiery manner: "The penalty for the lack of respect of proper law and order as evinced by vigilance committees and the Regulators of the West is still a yoke upon this nation, Mr. Bierce!"

"Our particular concern," Bierce said, "is with the vengeful efforts of those who had been exiled, or the partisans of those who were hanged by the Vigilance Committee— after they returned to San Francisco. As some did after a few years."

"My grandfather did not return," Miss Merkle said.

"Would he know of any instances?" Bierce asked.

"He is dead, Mr. Bierce. He died years ago—seven years ago. I will tell you on whom I might choose to wreak vengeance, if that were my nature."

"Who is that, Miss Merkle?"

"He is Mr. Brogan. He is a former president of the Bank of Nevada, and he was a member of the Committee. He was a very devil in my grandfather's situation."

"Yes, I know of Oliver Brogan," Bierce said.

There was a silence.

"If you will pardon me, Mr. Bierce, Mr. Redmond," Miss Merkle said in a tremulous voice. "My emotions are in a turmoil. You must pardon me . . ."

She gathered up her skirt and umbrella, settled her hat

and handbag, and swept to her feet, Bierce and I having risen with her.

"I am sorry, Miss Merkle——" Bierce started. We listened to the retreating clatter of her heels in the hall.

Bierce seated himself again. "I will pursue that young person further," he said. "She is very fetching, don't you think?"

SATURDAY, MARCH 26, 1892

My father came down from Sacramento for our monthly father-and-son dinner, for which he always paid with his ill-gotten gains from the Southern Pacific payroll. His stance was that Sacramento knew all that was going on in the "Evil City," as he called San Francisco. Over antipasti I brought up the subject of the Second Vigilance Committee.

He crunched his stem of celery, rolling an eye at me. "I was there!" he said.

"Proceed!" I said, although he needed no such encouragement.

"Well, at that time there was corruption aplenty in the Evil City. There was two branches of Democrats—the Chivs, for Southern Chivalry; and the Tammany boys, under Senator Broderick, who had brought the famous Improved Back-Action Ballot Box out from Manhattan. Double-bottomed, that is.

"There was two murder cases in jail at that time. There was Casey, who had shot James King dead in the street, no doubt about him. But Charlie Cora was another, earlier matter. He was a gambler, sure enough, and he kept company with Belle Ryan, who was beautiful and rich, and a madam for the gentry. They were sitting in the Bella Union watching a musicale, next to them the U.S. Marshal Richardson, whose wife was offended at sitting next to a scarlet woman and made a fuss about it. One thing led to another, so some days later the two men had a quarrel and Richardson threw down on Charlie Cora. Charlie drew faster, and shot him dead."

"Some question as to whether it was murder or self-defense," I said.

"So the jurymen thought, and hung up on the verdict. But James King made a great fuss that the jurors had been bought up by Belle Ryan."

He watched with sparkling eyes as the waiter poured red wine. He sipped, sighed, and continued:

"So then, when Casey was rightfully in jail for shooting James King, a mob stormed up to lynch him, and was held off by the sheriff. So the Vigilance Committee reconvened itself, and armed itself because a bunch of the membership were also members of the state militia and had militia rifles available. Six thousand men in all, I believe it was. That's a lot! They marched to the jail, demanded that the sheriff surrender Casey and Cora, and took them back to Fort Gunnybags and strung them up."

The waiter stood over us with his head bowed attentively. My father ordered for both of us, as was his way.

"Well, sir," he went on. "Here Governor Johnson had a first-class insurrection on his hands, and who was the general of militia but William Tecumseh Sherman! Sherman called up the militia from the rest of the state that had not gone in with the vigilantes, and the federal General Wool promised them arms. There was going to be blood running in the streets of San Francisco if the vigilantes did not disband!

"Just then, General Wool decided he could not turn over arms to the militia without authorization from Washington City. And Sherman, in a pure dudgeon, resigned from the matter."

"I'm sure marching through Georgia seemed easier," I said.

My father chuckled impatiently. "The Law and Order Party was thereupon formed to help the governor out against the outlaw stranglers. And guess who volunteered to that outfit! Your father, scarcely out of knee breeches!"

I regarded him with increased interest.

"Friend of mine named Rube Maloney recruited me and two others to take a shipment of a hundred or so rifles down the river aboard a schooner to the militia in the City. Well, sir, the vigilantes intercepted us—act of piracy! Took the rifles away and made us prisoners.

"There was some scuffling, as Rube Maloney was not one to surrender without a fuss. Come to help us out was militia from the City, and one of them was Judge David Terry of the California State Supreme Court. What did he do but knife one of the stranglers, name of Sterling Hopkins. So when the vigilantes marched us off to jail at Fort Gunnybags they had a tiger by the tail, for they had made a prisoner of a supreme court justice, and, if Hopkins died, by their own standards they were going to have to hang him.

"They let us go all except Terry, but Hopkins didn't die, so there was no doubt some relief when they let Terry go, too."

"Now, the stranglers had sworn they were only after murderers of a political order and ballot-box tamperers, and they would leave be the usual run of crimes—including, as they said, 'crimes of passion'—to the regular authorities.

"But they didn't. There was two crimes of passion murderers in jail. Took them out and hung them, too, and nothing the Law and Order people, who was me among them could do, but stand and watch.

"That August there was one more grand parade, those fools with their rifles on their shoulders pretending to be soldiers marching up and down—and it was all over."

I said, "After the Second Vigilance Committee was disbanded, the citizens who had been banished began to come back. I would think they would have had some grievances against the members of the Committee."

"Good reason for it," my father said, ingesting clam linguine.

"Would there still be some seeking revenge?"

He straightened, looking startled. "What are you saying?"

"Mrs. Potter thinks her husband was murdered by someone from his vigilante past rather than Oz Bird. Because another former vigilante, named Borland, was murdered in Roseville last week, she says."

"I'll look into it, Tommy," the gent said, going after his linguine again. He shook his head, "Think of that!" he said. "Borland?"

"You don't know a man in Roseville named Borland?" I asked, surprised. Roseville was not far from Sacramento.

"Don't know him," he said. "Murdered how?"

I didn't know that.

"Look into it," he said again. "You and Bierce working on this business, are you?"

"Oz Bird made specific death threats against Colonel Studely of the Wild West Show, and Arliff K. Potter of the Railroad," I said. "It may be that someone else took advantage of those threats."

"Think of that!" he said again. "Well, you and his nibs are two smart people!"

I listened for irony in his tone. He did not like Bierce because Bierce disapproved of too many things.

Over dessert he said, "Someone from years ago. That's thirty-six years. Why so long?"

"Maybe they just got out of prison, like Oz Bird. Or took the idea of revenge from him. And him to blame for it."

"Sounds a bit airy-fairy to me," my father said. "Maybe it wouldn't to Ambrose Bierce."

CHAPTER SIXTEEN

RENOWN, n. *A degree of distinction between notoriety and fame — a little more supportable than the one and a little more intolerable than the other. Sometimes it is conferred by an unfriendly and inconsiderate hand.*
— *The Devils's Dictionary*

SUNDAY, MARCH 27, 1892

On Sunday, in "Prattle," Bierce praised Miss "Miracle," inordinantly, I thought, for her performance in *Our American Cousin.* He had also written on the subject of Eugenics again:

> *One may be impressed by the warnings of the Eugenicists as to the dangers to the quality of the race of man from the careless poor, who will endow us with legions of paupers and the feeble-minded. But one is reassured by the inherent instinct of the female animal, who most willingly opens her bedcurtain to the wealthy, the powerful, and the ennobled, who, excepting the last, do tend to raise the quality of her offspring.*

In her female column, Miss Keith had written of the Ace of Shoots, praising Dora Pratt as Bierce had praised Miss

117

"Miracle," but much more long-windedly. I was particularly pleased by the end of the piece:

> . . . *How did this unassuming, shyly charming young woman become the second-best shot in the world? She is not merely the second-best female shot, she is the second-best shot. For reasons little understood and in certain circles much resented, the best of the Wild West Shows' wingshots are women. It is believed to be because of some feminine quality of serenity, of concentration, of focus. Miss Pratt is only five feet, two inches tall, but her small hands are very muscular and her left wrist is an inch larger in diameter than her right from holding her rifle leveled.*
>
> *She is a famous woman. She is a jewel of her gender. She is a woman respected and envied by persons of the other gender. This little lady, feet planted on the saddle of her trotting pony, rifle to her cheek, fires and explodes the glass balls which are thrown up before her, and has exploded the balls of prejudice and scorn thrown against her by the male gender, and has triumphed.*
>
> *How will she help her sisters to rise from their postures of servility before the hostile males who control their lives?*
>
> *"We will have the vote presently," says Miss Pratt, the Ace of Shoots, Little Miss Nevermiss, as she is also called. "That will even things a bit. And we who have not been permitted education, must take what education that comes, however it comes—as I have done. Our equality will surely follow!"*

I wished that I had written such a hymn of praise to Dora Pratt.

....

I was a fireman when I first came to San Francisco from Sacramento, and proud of it. I played on the firemen's baseball team in the City League, sometimes pitching, but more often as catcher, for I had a speedy and accurate throw to second base. Most of our games were played Sunday mornings on one of the diamonds in the park on Market Street. The Firemen wore red shirts, baggy knickers, and red stockings, some with bandannas or caps worn backward.

Today the fog was heavy, flowing between the buildings and seeming to squash them down, foghorns in their variety sounding off the Bay. The mist was so thick the outfielders looked dim and insubstantial, and fly balls lost themselves in the gray soup.

We put off starting the game against Bailey's Brewery until the fog had lightened a bit. Some early, bundled-up citizens, mainly gents, clustered together in the little cliff of grandstand. Two black-hatted men were seated higher than the others.

One of the louder foghorns sounded a long, low note and ceased. The Firemen were up.

Fred Jeeter got a base hit and stole second, and I came to bat. Squinting at the pitcher and jerking my club at him, I fouled one up the third baseline.

All at once the two men high in the stands were on their feet, one pointing, the other gawking. *Bird and Jukes*. Suddenly the bat weighed a hundred pounds.

I took a strike, a ball, another ball. I swung and connected, with a solid crunch in my arms. The ball sailed up into the fog.

I heard two shots, so close together they might almost have been one. The ball fluttered to earth like a shot duck.

Bird and Jukes were standing, and I saw the glint of a revolver in Bird's hand.

Brewers and Firemen stood as though frozen. Some of the firemen, seated on the bench, were rising; some remained seated. A foghorn bellowed.

Bird and Jukes tramped down the rows of plank seats, the other spectators lurching out of their way. Bird's revolver had disappeared inside his coat. He gazed at me steadily as he and his accomplice strolled past the silent players, and he raised one hand, his finger pointed at me, his thumb jerking once. Then he passed out on to Market Street and was gone.

He knew of my relation with Dora. *How did he know?*

"What the dickens was that about?" the Brewers' catcher asked.

"That was Oz Bird," I said. I was having trouble breathing.

"Christ almighty! What'd he do that for?"

"He was delivering a message," I said.

MONDAY, MARCH 28, 1892

In the morning, I had just turned into Bierce's office to tell him of the event at the ball game when Miss Keith popped in.

"I must tell you, Mr. Bierce, how gratified I was at your comments in yesterday's "Prattle" on the Eugenicists."

"Thank you, Miss Keith," he said. "And I was most impressed by your piece on the admirable Miss Pratt."

She thanked him in turn, and was gone.

"That woman is dangerous," he said to me. "She seems to agree with my most outrageous opinions, and sometimes I agree with hers! Often I withhold opinions, lest I find myself in further agreement."

"Including Calomel?" I said.

"I am persuaded by my own lack of faith in the perspicacity of doctors."

Mammy Pleasant bustled in just then, green-cloaked, a

covered basket under her arm. Bierce and I rose to our feet to greet her.

"Darkey Duncan," Mammy Pleasant said, gazing sideways at me. "Mr. Bierce thought I might be able to discover what hold Colonel Studely had on him. There was an attachment he had for a lady south of Market Street, name of Crystal. Crystal say he like to killed a man in St. Louis." She seated herself, placing her basket on the floor beside her.

"Continue, please," Bierce said. "Motive."

"Crystal say Darkey very attached to the shooter lady in Colonel Studely's Show."

"Miss Dora Pratt," I said. "Duncan is one of four men attached to her."

"Seems there was a fellow mashed on her in St. Louis. Followed the Show around and kep' turning up around her, trying to make up to her. Darkey didn't like it.

"Darkey took after him, give him a beating. Black men don't beat up on white men in St. Louis. Colonel Studely had connections that got him out of trouble."

I blew out my breath. I saw why I had had a communication from the Praetorians to the effect that my attentions to Miss Pratt had passed muster.

"Not that Darkey was much grateful to the colonel," Mammy said to Bierce. "Crystal say he say the colonel was a mean, tight-fisted devil of a man, outspoken of people's personal fault."

"Is there any information of Mr. Duncan's provenance?"

"What's that?"

"His origins."

"Born I don't know just where. Come west and work as a cowboy and rodeo fellow till the colonel hired him. Been in the Show four, five years, she say. Mighty attached to Miss Pratt."

"Anything of Guttman, Mrs. Pleasant?"

"I told you he put up in a rooming house on Second Street. He also roomed at Mrs. Cunningham's, in the same block on Third Street."

"That is new, then," Bierce said. "Mr. Redmond will look into it. Thank you so much, Mrs. Pleasant."

....

When Mammy had gone, Bierce said, "I do not inquire into your affairs, Tom, but it does seem that you have formed an attachment for Miss Pratt more considerable than that of confidant."

I told him of the incident at the ball game yesterday.

He propped his fingertips together again and whistled softly. He gazed down at his folded hands, his forehead creased with what I was pleased to realize was worry for me. "Tom, I am fearful that your relation with Miss Pratt may have been rendered more poignant by the threat of her former husband."

The threat of her husband was suddenly a part of my daily life.

CHAPTER SEVENTEEN

TREE, n. A tall vegetable intended by nature to serve as a penal apparatus, though through a miscarriage of justice most trees bear only a negligible fruit, or none at all. When naturally fruited, the tree is a beneficent agency of civilization and an important factor in public morals. In the stern West and the sensitive South its fruit (white and black respectively) though not eaten, is agreeable to the public taste and, though not exported, profitable to the general welfare.

— The Devil's Dictionary

TUESDAY, MARCH 29, 1892

The retired bank president, Oliver Brogan, was an old fellow with fat cheeks that quivered when he spoke and a head of silky white hair. His office on the second floor of his tall house on Leavenworth Street contained mahogany paneling, a desk, gas lamps on the walls, and a chandelier. I thought it might be a copy of the office he had captained at the Bank of Nevada. He did not rise to greet me, explaining that it took him such a long time to gain his feet that whoever was on hand would remember another engagement and depart. He was old, he pointed out.

The words *Second Vigilance Committee* were enough to get him started.

"We cleaned out the sinners from the City, young man. Took some doing!" He knitted his fingers together and rocked a little.

"Most people who were on hand speak well of it," I said.

"Citizens were for it—ninety percent for it."

"Most people speak well of it," I said again. "Except, perhaps, the lynchings."

His features concentrated into a scowl. "What lynchings was that, young man?"

"Cora and Casey. Especially Cora."

"Lynching is what they do to Negroes in the South. It is a barbarous practice. Those men were tried before a court of their peers."

"Well, sir, a court of their peers, but they had no opportunity to bring witness in their behalf—"

"Young man," Brogan interrupted, frowning heavily. "I see you are unclear about the differences between a lynching in the South and an extreme sanction by the Vigilance Committee in San Francisco."

"Well, sir," I said politely, "they are both illegal acts, are they not?"

"Let me make a comparison," he said, in such a way that I believed it was a comparison he had made many times before in just such an explanation as this.

"One day I cross my neighbor's field. It is not an illegal act. The next day, he has put up a NO TRESPASSING sign, and it becomes an illegal act. But wait! What if one man is trying to murder another man in that field and I trespass to prevent that murder from taking place? Can we say that I have committed an illegal act to prevent an evil act? Do you follow me, young man?"

I followed him.

"I repeat that lynching Negroes in the South is barbarous and against the law, but that by hanging such criminals as Casey and Cora we sought to establish civilization in what had become a barbarous city."

"Of course that is true, sir. But both acts defy law and order."

"Do they, in fact?"

"Well, sir, I believe citizens taking the law into their own hands does that."

He looked pleased, as though in a chess game I had made a fatal wrong move. "Ordinary citizens, indeed! And from whose hands do those ordinary citizens take the law?"

"From the elected officials."

"And who elected those officials, if not the ordinary citizens?"

"That is true," I said, my fingers crossed in my lap.

"You see, young man, in the South, when they take a Negro from the jail, there is no probability that he will *not* be hanged for his crimes by the elected officials. The South has never claimed that the law would let him go. The courts in San Francisco had been letting such criminals and murderers go for many years. The courts—into whose hands we had put our law—the judges, and the juries were not dealing the law. They were corrupt hands. They were hands that grasped for money instead of dealing law. So when the ordinary citizen sees this, he must take the law back from those corrupt hands, into his own hands.

"Far from being a defiance of the law, this is an assertion of it—the fundamental assertion of self-governing men, upon whom our whole social fabric is based. That was the principle of the Second Vigilance Committee, young man. Is it Mr. Redding?"

"Redmond, sir," I said. "That is very clearly put, Mr. Brogan."

His face creased in self-congratulation. I thought that his

speech had been perfected among ordinary citizens who had been loath to challenge an old man's rationalizations.

"Tell me, Mr. Brogan: Some of these criminals were hanged, but most were merely deported. Did not some of these return, seeking satisfaction? The names of the men of the Vigilance Committee were widely publicized."

"Indeed they were," Brogan said. "That also is a difference, you see. No concealment behind white robes and masks. Yes, indeed, there were lawsuits, and certainly some threats of violence. That had to be dealt with."

I inquired how these had been dealt with.

"Well, there was an executive committee, you understand. We hired a young man to deal with those threats."

"Counter-threats?" I asked.

He laughed and slapped his knee.

"He would have given anyone pause, that young man. He was a fellow with a reputation, and a deadly aspect."

The word *deadly* reminded me of Mrs. Potter's description.

"Was his name Ike Guttman?" I asked.

I thought I had a hit, but he said, "The name will remain a secret as far as I am concerned!"

"Thank you for your time, and for your very clear explanation, Mr. Brogan," I said, rising.

He bent to ring the spittoon. "Just a moment, Mr. Redding," he said. "That name you mentioned—how did you come by it?"

"Coincidence," I said. "Another context. Someone spoke of him as looking like death."

"And who would that be, young man?"

"That will have to be my secret, sir."

"That is indeed the name of the man to whom I referred. Probably he has passed to his reward," Brogan said, knitting his fingers together again. "So many, many years ago!"

I took my hat from the hook behind the door and left the old vigilante's office.

....

The address on Third Street was on the Bay side, halfway down the block, a square three-story structure with a sign in a downstairs window: ROOMS. I mounted six steps and cranked the bell. The door was promptly opened about eight inches, and a severe female face under a mob-cap gazed out at me.

"Are you the proprietor, madam?" I asked.

"Mrs. Cunningham's the proprietor. She's sick."

"I'm interested in a tenant who lived here about eight years ago."

"Oh, you mean that Guttman person?" She opened the door a little wider.

"What do you know of him?" I said.

"Fellow was here yesterday asking about him. Come on in. Mrs. Cunningham's bedsick, but she talked to him, she can talk to you."

Mrs. Cunningham lay abed in the room with the ROOMS sign in the window, just to the right, inside the front door. She sat up, yellow-faced, gray-haired, and with a knit cap on against stacked pillows.

"Here's another one asking about that Guttman," the maid said.

"Was his name Burgess?" I asked.

"I've got his card here somewhere; Fred Jones I think it was. Lanky young fellow with some fair beard to him."

"Fred Jones," I said, nodding. "And what could you tell him about Ike Guttman?"

"Not much," Mrs. Cunningham said, batting a feeble hand at the pillows that supported her. "I surely don't remember that gentlemen. I don't even have the guest register from that far back. Pale little gent is all I can remember, very polite, didn't say much. Kept his hat on when he was inside, which, because he had better manners than that, made me wonder if he didn't have a bald head he was ashamed to show. Never did see him hat off. Went off leaving some things of his'n in the basement closet, as I already told Mr. Jones."

I asked about the things left in the basement closet.

"Box about the size of a big hatbox, leather. Some mold to it; it is damp down there!"

I wondered if I might see the box.

"Oh, Mr. Jones carried if off. He was kin, you see. Said that was what he'd come for, Mr. Guttman old and ailing down south somewhere. So I let him take it."

"Thank you very much, Mrs. Cunningham," I said, and left feeling as though I'd been thrown out at home plate.

....

Jake Burgess ushered me into his cubicle at the *Chronicle,* where three desks were crowded together, one of them his.

"Not much in it," he said. He opened his second drawer and took out a rusty derringer, an empty whiskey bottle, a Jew's harp, a fingernail file, a brush with a missing back, and an accordion fold of postcards hinged together—views of St. Louis.

"This is all there was," Jake said. "All the clues you and Bierce could dream of."

He held out the postcards. The top one had been torn off; the second was a colored view of the railroad station. This was addressed to Mrs. Eulalia Watson, 17 Claude Street, St. Louis, Missouri.

"Isn't any Claude Street in St. Louis," Jake said.

"How do you know?"

"They've got city maps downstairs. Don't the *Examiner?* You think Claude connects to somebody's name? McGee and me can't figure out a thing from this."

Jake carried the postcards over to the light, manipulating the top one until indented printing was visible. I could make out some of what was written, the latter part of a message: "what I will not is dispose of an idiot booby for you, you son of a bitch."

I spoke the words. There were no others on the pad.

"Booby," Jake said.

He and Marshall McGee didn't know what was meant by it, either.

I held up my hands, empty. "Thanks for cutting me in, Jake," I said.

"I didn't think I was cutting you in on anything you can use," he said. "Don't tell me if I'm wrong."

....

At the Fairgrounds, Dora was not in evidence as I turned in past the grandstand, where the unhitched old Concord hung on its thoroughbraces. Billy Buttons rode up to me, waving his hat toward the barn.

"She's in there, shootin'."

I continued on to the barn, where indeed I could hear muffled shots. Just inside was a ladder to the hayloft, and I climbed its seven rungs and made my way along the aisle in the loft between bales of hay in the dusty dark. The shots had ceased.

At the back of the barn the hayloft stopped, and in a high, brighter space there I could see, below me, Dora and a man standing together. A dusty, many-paned window let in some light, and the man's stance was so distinctive that I halted. It was Bierce, wearing a soft hat. Both he and Dora had their right arms extended, their revolvers pointing to the floor. Opposite them, a bale of hay was plastered with paper targets. Dora wore a kind of dungaree coverall from which her white-sleeved arms extended.

Bierce was talking: "I acquired it when the admirer of a

young actress whose performance I had criticized assaulted me in my office."

"But you have not fired it?" Dora asked.

"I have come to you for instruction."

"Very well," Dora said. She sounded brisk and instructional. "Try number six."

Bierce raised his revolver awkwardly before his face and fired. They both regarded the target. I couldn't see if he had hit it or not.

"It is difficult," Bierce said, "to fit the blade of the front sight into the V of the rear one."

"Please try this," Dora said. "Just lay your finger along the barrel and point your finger. That's right. Now, number eight."

Bierce raised the revolver, not so high this time, and fired again.

"That is better, Mr. Bierce!"

"Thank you, Miss Pratt."

"There are some matters to understand. Whatever gun you have is to be *permitted* to fire. To do this, you release the trigger. You do not impel the firing, you permit it."

"Is that so?"

"As you have seen, the muzzle will kick up with each shot. You must take the time to bring it down and level the barrel, pointing. You will be surprised at how accurate your pointing will become. Now: number three and number seven."

Bierce fired twice.

Reloading with cartridges taken from his pocket, he said, "That is much more comfortable, Miss Pratt."

"Number two and number five."

Twice more, dust plumed in little puffs from the bale of hay.

Dora stood facing him, her arms folded on her breast. She had holstered her own weapon.

"You are in control," she continued in her schoolmarm voice. "It is the desire of your weapon to fire. It is you who permit it to fire. You see, it is the other way around from what you might think."

"You endow the weapon with the human quality of desire, do you, Miss Pratt?"

"I know guns very well, Mr. Bierce. Now: eight and five."

He fired, with more of a pause between shots.

I was uncomfortable in my role as eavesdropper, and it seemed awkward now to call attention to myself, so I retreated along the hayloft aisle in the dusty air. There were more shots as the lesson continued.

Outside the barn I encountered Billy Buttons again, dismounted this time.

"She is giving my friend Mr. Bierce a shooting lesson," I said.

"It'll be a good one!" Billy said, beaming. "She is a nonesuch, she is!"

I agreed with him.

"I have known her longer than anybody but Robbie Studely and Lawyer Boxcroft," he said.

"So you knew Bird."

"That was a fellow with a lot of hard bark on him." He grinned and scuffed a boot. "*Is,* I guess. When's she gonna be done in there, you think?"

I said I had no idea about that, and he traipsed off, whistling in a monotone. I headed for the Jacal to wait for the conclusion of the instruction of Ambrose Bierce as a shootist.

When I saw Bierce again he was carrying the colonel's big parrot in a complicated wire cage. Ted let out a muted squawk at seeing me.

"Boxcroft has sent the perfect Mrs. Dierdorf packing," Bierce said. "There is no evidence of the loan to her golden boy she spoke of, although Boxcroft thinks it likely enough the money was borrowed. I had the sense that Mr. Boxcroft is as tough as a Turk in financial matters. Some unpleasantness resulted, apparently."

He did not mention his shooting instruction.

He had borrowed Ted, he said, holding the cage up higher so I could meet the parrot's gaze, for an interrogation session in his office.

CHAPTER EIGHTEEN

REPORT, n. *A rumor. The sound of a firearm.*
"Why did you not march to my relief, sir?" said General Ewell to the com-
mander of one of his divisions. "Did you not hear the report of the guns?"
"Well, yes, General, I did hear the report, but I didn't believe it."
— The Devil's Dictionary

TUESDAY, MARCH 29, 1892

Later, when I dropped into Bierce's office, Ted was out of his
cage, clawed onto a chair back next to the desk. The bird eyed
me as I entered, first with one eye, then the other, and displayed
a gray wad of tongue.

"How has the interview with Ted gone?"

"It is rather like playing chess blindfolded," Bierce said, his
fingers tented together. "There are the colonel's and Miss
Pratt's voices, and another that must be Mr. Boxcroft's.
Miss Pratt evidently said, 'But Robbie—' a good deal, and Ted
has taken that up. Also 'Rocks and shoals,' in the colonel's
voice. 'Where's Percy?' 'Where's Evalina?' and 'Where's
Dory?' seem to be constructions of his own, not mimicked.
The colonel apparently repeated excoriations enough times
for Ted to pick up on them. 'Fraud! Pisspot!' " He frowned

at a list on his desk. " 'Idiot! Moron! Booby!' Were these directed at Miss Pratt, or at Boxcroft? Or at Ted himself, for some misbehavior?"

Ted stepped carefully sideways on his chair back. He had not yet taken an eye off me.

There was a legend of Bierce having an affinity for birds, or of birds for him. I smothered a grin to think of birds coming to rest on his shoulders, like St. Francis, and of Ted revealing *all*.

"Where's Evalina?" I said. Ted waddled two steps to the right, but did not respond.

"Where's Evalina?" Bierce said. Ted glanced at him briefly, but still did not reply.

"Who's the idiot?" Bierce said.

Ted kept his eye fixed on me.

"We were having quite a lively chat," Bierce said. "Now he seems to have gone mute."

"I'll go along, then."

Bierce said, "Do you suppose Ted is aware of your interest in Miss Pratt? Do birds have intuition? Certainly animals are capable of jealousy."

"Maybe he knows I am having dinner with Miss Pratt at the Cliff House tonight," I said and departed, feeling curiously miffed.

....

That evening, gazing out on the moonlit Seal Rocks from a window in the Cliff House, Dora and I feasted on steak and quail, slick little potatoes, and salad, with a claret of some quality to wash it down.

The world's second-best wingshot, who was rarely recognized because she always performed in her schoolgirl dress, was quiet and, habitually, a little sad. I had important matters to discuss with her but something, maybe anxiety, hung over this evening like a dull mist.

Heading back to the City on the steam train, Dora and I sat in one of the rear seats, gazing out at the moonlight on the lunar wilderness of sand dunes.

She leaned against me. The warmth of her released my paralyzed tongue.

"Dora?"

"Tom."

"What will you do now?"

"I have been meaning to ask you that. What you will you do?"

"I will be a journalist for the *Examiner* newspaper, Dora."

She stretched, achieving a little more contact. "I don't think I am competent to run Rob Studely's Wild West Show."

"Hire someone to run it."

"Do you know what I have dreamt?"

I thought I knew what she had dreamt, and it was my nightmare. "I can't become a kind of house journalist for the Show, Dora."

"Must I become a housewife for a San Francisco *Examiner* journalist?"

I put my arm around her, and she snuggled her head against my chin. She smelled of flowers. The car crackety-cracked, swaying, along the rails across the sand hills. The moon picked out a single straggly tree against a pale dune.

"How did Evalina die?" I asked.

"She died because she wasn't allowed to live. She died because she was born dying." She was silent for a time. "What do children die of? She was never well. She would never have been well. We had boarded her with a nurse who was careless, and her little light went out. Was it my fault, then? Of course; it is always the parents' fault! Never mind it, Tom. I do not wish to speak of her!"

I squeezed her against me. "I'm sorry."

"I am tired of guns, and shooting," she said. "And people dead of guns and shooting, which is such a part of guns and shooting. I am tired of dressing like a schoolgirl. I am tired of my life."

"I don't think you are tired of being the second-best shooter in the world."

"Maybe I am!" she whispered.

She might, at this moment, think that she was.

The train rocked along eastward toward the City, a distant pale glow in the sky that was not the moon. In the front of the car a man and a woman were arguing in loud voices, which irritated me out of proportion.

"I don't think we are being guarded tonight," I said.

She shook her head against me.

"What I would like," I said, "is to take you in hand. I would like to get rid of the sadness that rides you so hard, but yet is a part of your very person. Surely you must forget the sadness of Evalina sometime! I would change you into the happy person I know is inside there somewhere!"

"I would like that so much!"

She asked about my salary at the *Examiner*.

"It is not large," I said.

"The Show makes quite a lot of money. Rob lived well. He didn't pay anyone well."

I knew that.

"Buffalo Bill would pay me twice as much. More than that— he wants an ongoing competition with Annie Oakley. You know, if we did that, I would beat her eventually."

"You see?" I said.

"I have some money," she said.

"That's not the point."

"No."

"What will happen to the Show now?"

"It will go on, unless I go to Buffalo Bill."

"Would it collapse if you left it?"

"I don't know." She took several deep breaths. "I am a widow twice. I have been with two men who were my instructors. What would you be, Tom?"

"Not an instructor."

"You could instruct me in good food and drink."

"I don't want to instruct you in anything."

"I like your Miss Keith," she said, changing the subject.

"She is not my Miss Keith. She may be Bierce's poetry pupil."

"She talked of Hull-House in Chicago. Helping the immigrant women and children. It sounded such a wonderful, useful place."

I felt a pang of jealousy I had never felt when she spoke of her husbands.

"Miss Keith is a feminist, and you are a celebrated wingshot," I said.

"I don't know what I am, Tom," she said.

The train slowed, chuffing, into the station on Presidio Street. There was no question that Dora would come to my rooms with me this night, but what then?

....

Several times in her transports, Dora, panting, grasped my arms in her strong hands and stared into my eyes, stared into my eyes as though searching for something there, as though searching for something but not finding it.

I bristled with resentment for whatever the inadequacy she found in me, the lack she found in me, the disappointments of her search.

It seemed that everything I wrote for the *Examiner* about the murders of Studely and Potter was affected by my intimacies with her. I had become Dora Pratt's journalist more than the *Examiner*'s.

When I told her of Oz Bird's appearance at the ball game, and his shot, and the snapping pistol of his hand, she laid her head on my chest, still breathing hard. I thought she must be weeping, but she was not weeping.

"It was always that way," she said in a muffled voice. "He knew what I'd been doing! Even when he would write me from prison, it was as though he knew. So he must know about us!"

"I know I must be very careful. But he may want to go on with his memoirs."

"I think he likes being in the newspaper. Tom, won't they catch him *soon?*"

"Did you consider yourself married to Studely?"

"Mr. Boxcroft says I must claim to be a common-law wife."

"But you and he . . . were no longer connected."

"Mr. Boxcroft says that doesn't matter."

"You will inherit the Show. Is that what you want?"

"I don't know. I just don't want it to go to smash."

"I don't mean to interrogate you," I said.

I took her back to her hotel, waving a hand in greeting out of the hack in case one of her Praetorians was guarding us against Oz Bird.

I had to catch the early train for Sacramento; I was to meet my father and head for Roseville to look into the death of a man named Borland, in case Oz Bird had not murdered Arliff K. Potter or Colonel Studely.

CHAPTER NINETEEN

FEMALE, n. One of the opposing, or unfair, sex.
— The Devil's Dictionary

WEDNESDAY, MARCH 30, 1892

Roseville was north of Sacramento, in flat country. The California Geological Survey had done the Central Pacific Railroad the favor of classifying the area as mountainous so the Big Four would receive triple the flat-land construction rate on building their line there. In my father's SP buggy we drove along the level rail line in brilliant sun as the early fog melted away around us.

"I was thinking about what was said last time I saw you," my father said. "We were talking about David Terry."

I knew a good deal about David Terry.

"Shot Broderick in a duel," he went on. "Murdered him, some said. There was such a fuss over it, Terry had to leave the state.

"When he come back he was hired to help out Sarah Althea Hill in her case against Senator Sharon. She had been Sharon's kept woman and claimed he had married her, which he claimed he had not. It was in both state court and federal court, since Sharon was the senator from Nevada."

"Terry got to be her loverman, then they married. They won the state case and began to rejoice, but the federal case had still to run, and the judge was an old Comstock pal of Sharon's. Should have recused himself! Name of Field; he'd also been a supreme court justice along with David Terry. Well, Judge Field found against Sarah Althea and David Terry, and they were shipwrecked. You can bet David Terry was laying for Judge Field! So Judge Field got him a bodyguard, name of Dave Neagle.

"Terry caught up with him in a railroad station down by Fresno and went after him with his bowie knife. Dave Neagle shot him dead."

"Yes," I said. "Someone like that."

"You don't have a name yet?"

"Maybe it's Guttman," I said.

....

The Borland place was off a rutted track that ran along the edge of a gulch, past cornfields thick with green stalks. Sheriff Ruster of Placer County did not know much about the Borlands, my father had told me; they had moved there only months ago, to the old Peyton ranch. Nobody had seen much of them. Borland had been shot by two men on horseback, who had called him out, had some words with him, and plugged him. His wife had seen it but hadn't heard the content of the exchange, except that it had to do with somebody from back in the vigilante days, when Borland had been active on the Second Vigilance Committee.

The curious thing, the sheriff had told my father, was that Mrs. Borland had washed her husband's body and dressed it in Sunday-go-to-meeting, all ready for his funeral, which had taken place the next day with no one but her and the parson in attendance since they had no acquaintances in the district.

There was a severe dip in the road where it crossed the

gulch, and I jumped out so the horse could pull the buggy up the far side. The Borland house was dilapidated, board-sided with a patch of missing shingles, a brick chimney, and white paint peeling off the two columns that supported the porch roof. Chickens scratched around the yard, and a fat woman came out to the porch to gaze at us with her hands tucked in to her apron. Her hair was glossy, brown, and thick. Beneath it was a piggish face set in pugnacious lines.

"Whatcher want?" she called out.

I walked toward her while my father wound the buggy whip around its handle.

"We would like to speak to you about your husband's death, Mrs. Borland."

"Who are you?"

I explained that I was a journalist with the San Francisco *Examiner*.

"Told it to Sheriff Ruster."

"If we could have a few moments of your time."

With a noticeable lack of graciousness we were allowed to seat ourselves on the porch, which resulted in our being jammed together on a bench, facing her. She wore a stained apron over a flowered dress, and gray gum boots. She kept pushing and tucking at what was surely a wig.

"Your husband was a member of the Vigilance Committee of eighteen fifty-six?" I asked her.

"That's what he told me."

"And he made lifelong enemies?"

"He was the one managed the rope when they hanged one of those brutes." She had a high, thick voice that made me want to clear my own throat.

"Which one? Casey? Cora?"

"It wasn't them; it was some other."

"And the men who shot your husband had to do with that?"

"He was always afraid somebody was coming after him. We moved around a good bit. He'd get spooked, and we'd move on again. Poor way to live."

"But he never said from whom the threat might be?"

She shook her head, which necessitated more adjustments to her wig.

"Never talked about it," she said. "Never talked about any of it. Just somebody after him. Well, they caught up with him at last, leavin' me here to run this place alone."

"You have no children, madam?" my father asked.

"Never had none. Henry had two boys by his first wife."

"And where would they be?"

She thought one was in Colorado, one back east. Her husband had not kept track of them. She gazed off toward town, one eye slitted against a ray of sun. My father had picked up a small stone, which he tossed up and caught several times in what I found to be an irritating manner.

" 'Fraid there's not much I can tell you gents," Mrs. Borland said. "You talk to Sheriff Ruster; I told him all I know."

My father flipped the little stone up again. This time, it spun too far and landed in Mrs. Borland's lap.

"Sorry, madam," he said. "Got away from me."

Scowling, she brushed the stone from her apron. My father rose.

"I think we'd better go speak to the sheriff as the lady says, Tommy."

He set off down the three rickety steps, and there was nothing for me to do but follow him. Mrs. Borland sat watching us go. When he had swung the buggy around, I looked back to see that she had disappeared into the black rectangle of the doorway.

"She's no lady," my father chuckled.

"That is surely a wig."

"You remember in that Sam Clemens book, when Aunt Polly flips a thimble into Tom Sawyer's lap and knows he's a boy because he catches it by jamming his legs together instead of stretching them apart to catch it in his apron?"

I almost shouted with laughter. "That's what you did!"

"That's what I did," he said, pleased with himself. He had known Sam Clemens in Virginia City on the Comstock, and had read all of Mark Twain's novels, surely the only novels he did read.

"I expect that was Mr. Borland, son," he said.

"So that's why he washed and dressed the body and put the Sunday clothes on," I said. "What's it all about?"

"The sheriff better know of it, anyway."

"Murdered his wife, and claimed it had to do with the old vigilante days?"

"Wouldn't want to speculate," my father said, who had just proved himself a better detective than his son.

....

Sheriff Ruster was surely interested in what we had to say. We were seated together outside his office on the boardwalk on Roseville's main street, among a clatter of passing wagons. "That explains why she dressed him up like that!" he said. "Because it was *him* dressing *her* up like that. I do thank you, Clete," he said to my father.

My father made some show of lighting a cigar.

"Isn't Oz Bird from around here, Sheriff?" I asked.

"Just north of here a bit," he said, nodding. "The old Guttman place. We are watching for that fellow!"

"The *Guttman* place?"

"The Guttmans and the Birds were connected; I forget just

how. Married to each other, or some such. The old ones are all dead now."

The realization was like a slap in the face: Guttman and Bird, Gizzard and Buzzard.

"Seems I recall that the widow Guttman married Jake Bird," he continued. "Kits by different husbin. Bad conduct old female, too."

"Two boys?" I said.

"Well, I can't recall. There was half brothers and nephews and such kin all jammed together in the old Guttman place. Young ones and old ones."

"Did you hear of an Ike Guttman?"

He shook his head, frowning.

"Oz Bird's in San Francisco," I said. "I wonder where Ike Guttman is?"

"Wouldn't know that. Not around here, anyhow."

....

In the home of my youth in Sacramento, which still reeked slightly of mud from the river flooding years back, my mother's house slippers slapped along the hallway, and she flung herself into my arms. "Did you find out what you needed to know?"

"Found out something we didn't need to know," my father grumbled.

We seated ourselves in the parlor, such familiar surroundings that I raised my arms straight up and stretched mightily in comfort.

"I made a connection I needed to make," I said. "Buzzard and Gizzard must be half brothers, or uncle and nephew—kin, anyway, even if they weren't at Hungry Valley together."

"You'll have to explain that, Tommy," my mother said.

I explained.

"You are courting a Wild West Show shooter lady?" my mother asked incredulously.

"I don't think courting is the right word," I said. I must not frighten her with the threat of Oz Bird.

"Trust my son to beau a young lady with a rifle in her hand," my father said.

This introduced the subject of my mother's desire for a grandchild, which was a deep hole for me to clamber out of.

....

It was late and I was weary when I returned to San Francisco. I took a hack to the corner of Sacramento and Pine and paid off the hackie in the heavy darkness there so I could walk down the last block and pull my thoughts together. Streetlights glowed on the corners leading down toward Market Street, one of them across the street from my rooming house.

A man's silhouette was entangled with the lamp post in such a position of tension that I felt the hairs at the back of my neck bristle. I retreated to peer around the corner of the brick building nearest me.

I had no doubt it was Bird. In the dim light, the length of his rifle barrel glistened. I watched the glisten rise to a horizontal position beneath the black hat.

My eye was caught by a movement on my stoop, someone coming out of *my* door, a big hat outlined in the little light there. It was as though I saw myself coming out of my door, reaching back to test the door handle, while across the street beneath the light the long glisten had steadied and remained perfectly motionless. As the figure came down my steps I had an impulse to shout a warning, but my throat was paralyzed. I raised a hand as though to signal. As my double came off the steps to the sidewalk, the rifle crashed.

I watched myself spin on the sidewalk, my hat falling off,

one hand reaching down to break my fall, and then suddenly
flat on the sidewalk, motionless.

Beneath the streetlight, Oz Bird was one moment there, and
the next gone into shadows.

I remained frozen at the corner, gazing down at my shadowy
self prone on the sidewalk. I shook my head to clear it. There
was no sign of Bird now, who had shot me, trading his biogra-
phy for vengeance. I started at a trot down the sidewalk toward
the figure there.

He lay with his head toward the street, one arm out and the
other trapped under his body, his hat ten feet away, his blood
like a denser shadow on the ground beneath him. He wore a
black coat and a checked shirt. I bent to peer at the side of his
face, which was exposed to me. Enrique Garza had come out of
my rooms to be shot by Oz Bird, who had meant to kill me.

I hurried toward Market Street in search of a patrolman.

After an hour with the patrolman, and presently two detectives, trying to make sense of what I had seen, Enrique Garza's
body was loaded aboard a wagon and carted to the city morgue
out on Broadway.

At last I trudged up the five steps to my rooms, unlocked my
door, and turned the switch. Electric light from the central bulb
on its twisted cord filled the room. On top of my typewriter, a
white slip of paper stood up like an ear. It was a note from
Dora, which Garza had died to deliver:

> *Tom: Oz was here, watching me practice from
> over the fence. He saw that I saw him. I think you
> must stay out of it. It is for me to deal with. I will
> do what I must. Dora.*

I hurried to her hotel to hold her while she raged and
wept. She'd told Garza where I hid the key, behind the broken

brick, so that he could leave her note where I would be sure to
see it.

THURSDAY, MARCH 31, 1892

The morning headlines read

MISS PRATT CHALLENGED

....

SGT. MAULE WILL TRY HIS SKILLS

....

VETERAN RIFLEMAN AT PRESIDIO

....

Miss Pratt had accepted the challenge.

In my office was an urgent message to see Marshall McGee
of the *Chronicle*.

CHAPTER TWENTY

INHUMANITY, n. *One of the signal and characteristic qualities of humanity.*

— *The Devil's Dictionary*

THURSDAY, MARCH 31, 1892

McGee had a big third-floor office in the *Chronicle* building looking up Kearny Street toward Chinatown. Jake Burgess was with him. When I came in, they both switched around, blank-faced, as though I might be a visiting timberwolf.

"Mr. Redmond," McGee said. "We have had a visitation."

"What's that?"

"Guttman," Jake Burgess said.

"With what message?" I asked.

"Lay off."

"Lay off what?"

"Lay off him."

"Did he want his hatbox back?"

"He doesn't want his name appearing in the newspaper. Wondered if he'd come to see you and Bierce."

"He hasn't."

"He is a sick man," McGee said. He leaned back in his chair.

"White as paper, skinny as a snake, coughing his guts up. He's old!"

"I'll tell you, Tom," Burgess said. "That is one scary little man."

"Did he have a weapon?"

"Didn't need a weapon; breathe on you, you'd die of the plague."

"Going to be frank with you, Tom—no games," McGee said. "Whatever kind of animal it is that's a little killing machine—lynx, weasel, one of those—that is what Guttman is. He's an assassin. That's what he did for the Vigilantes when they were getting threats and lawsuits. They'd send Guttman over. He didn't have to kill anybody. He didn't even have to show a weapon. Desist!"

He leaned forward. "I don't even know if I can describe the effect he had on Jake and me. It was like seeing a cobra coming in the door. That little, white-faced, skinny fellow!"

"Assassin with a conscience," I said. "He didn't want to kill some booby, whatever that means."

McGee and Burgess looked at each other. Burgess turned to me.

"What it looks to us, Tom, this Guttman was the partner to Oz Bird in the Hungry Valley shoot-up."

"They might be kin," I said.

They looked at each other again.

"Detective work," Burgess said. McGee shook his head.

"Tom, how do you suppose Oz Bird likes you doobooleedo with his ex-wife?"

"I don't even know what that word means."

"What he shot Studely for."

"Tom, you are in a fix!" McGee said.

These two did not know that the Guttman at Hungry Valley

had been Dora Pratt, not Bird's kinsman. They seemed determined that Oz Bird, not one of the guardians, had shot Studely. And they were perfectly right that I was in a fix.

"Last night he shot a fellow, that he thought was me, coming off my stoop," I said. "It was Enrique Garza, from the Wild West Show."

"Thought it was you!" McGee said.

"I heard about that!" Jake said. "I didn't know it was at your place."

"Maybe you ought to take a long trip somewheres, Tom," McGee said.

I went back to the *Examiner* to inform Bierce. He had his hat on, ready for some detective work. "Here we go!" he said.

Rincon Hill had been split in half when Second Street was cut through, but St. Mary's Hospital still stood precariously there, and it was where Bierce had directed the hackie without any explanation to me as to why we were bound there.

One of the first-floor wings was for tuberculars, and Bierce engaged the nurse, a plump, tall, Irish-faced woman with fair hair wisping out from under her starched cap.

"He will be here somewhere," Bierce said to her. "A small man in his sixties with a very white face and a good deal of personal force."

"They's all small here," the nurse said. "Sucks the size right out of them. Personal force? That'd be Mr. Richards."

Coughs resounded through the high-ceilinged chamber as we moved among the cots toward a sunny patio. There we found three patients in cots folded into lounge chairs, white-faced invalids in the thin sun above the South Bay.

"Here's visitors, Mr. Richards," the nurse said as we halted before the last lounger.

Ike Guttmann stared up at us with furious eyes.

"Who's these people, Miss O'Malley?"

"My name is Bierce," Bierce said, standing at military atten
tion, in the way he did when he felt stress. "This is my associate,
Mr. Redmond. We are employed by the *Examiner* newspaper.
We are investigating the death of Colonel Studely."

"Nothing to do with me," Guttman said.

"I am aware of that, Mr. Guttman. There are peripheral
matters you can clear up, however."

"Why should I clear up anything, mister?"

Bierce folded his arms on his chest. "Why not, sir? I expect
you will not leave this place alive, from the look of you."

This unexpectedly caused Guttman to grin. His face was as
white as a marshmallow, with the up-curved split of his grin
like a dark gap in it. When the grin vanished he looked merely
old and sick.

"About correct, innit, Miss O'Malley?"

"We'll do our best to make it incorrect, Mr. Richards!"

"Could these undertakers here have chairs, then?"

Chairs were produced and Nurse O'Malley departed. Guttman regarded us with his intense eyes.

"Two old men who were members of the Second Vigilance
Committee have died in the last several weeks," Bierce proceeded. "Our competitors from the *Chronicle* newspaper think
you may be involved. We think you are not."

"Did some work for the Committee," Guttman said. He
cleared his throat hugely, coughing deeply. His forehead turned
pink for a moment, then returned to its dead white pallor.

"We will not inquire what was involved," Bierce said. "Other
than that you were hired to dissuade those who had claims
against the Committee from legal action."

"Something like that," Guttman said hoarsely.

"You were the Gizzard of Buzzard and Gizzard in the Hungry Valley matter. But you were not the person who accompanied Oswald Bird there."

Guttman was silent.

"You were in jail in San Francisco at that time! I have seen the records."

"Anybody go along with Ozzie on a play like that was sick in the head," Guttman said.

"What of Arliff Potter?" Bierce said.

"I knew Arlie Potter some. Ozzie shot him, dint he?"

"You knew him from vigilante days."

"That's right." He coughed into a big handkerchief and looked at Bierce and me, bright-eyed.

"I'm trying to get some glimmer of what you want from me, gents."

"Information," Bierce said.

"To my detriment."

"I assure you, no. Mr. Guttman, it may not have occurred to you, but no one can do anything to you that nature will not take her precedence."

The grin split the marshmallow face again. "It has occurred to me plenty," he said. "So, go on."

"St. Louis," Bierce said. "Something happened there, or didn't happen."

"Didn't happen by me," Guttman snapped.

One of the other tuberculars on the little porch had lit a cigarette and was lying with his head back and his face up to the sun with what was such obvious pleasure that I almost envied him.

"To a 'booby,' " Bierce said. "What does that mean, please?"

The hard blue eyes glared at him. "Means somebody stupid, as far as I know."

"I believe you were hired to do in a booby and resigned from it in good conscience."

"You don't know a durn thing about my conscience," Guttman said. He closed his eyes and laid his head back, as though exhausted. He cleared his throat hugely, and muttered, "Go away."

Bierce said, "If you will not help us, we will be forced to look elsewhere, which *could* be to your detriment."

"I don't have no detriment, like you said," Guttman replied.

"Mr. Guttman—" Bierce started, but Guttman began to cough, wet and deep. A splash of blood stained his white cheek. Bierce stood up and stepped back.

"Get Miss O'Malley!" one of the other patients called out.

Guttman's eyes opened, a cast of triumph in them as he coughed blood. I ran for the nurse.

CHAPTER TWENTY-ONE

BATTLE, n. *A method of untying with the teeth a political knot that would not yield to the tongue.*
— *The Devil's Dictionary*

THURSDAY, MARCH 31, 1892

At the Fairgrounds I hoped to see Dora alone before her match with the Presidio sergeant, but she was seated in the Jacal with the remaining three of her guard—Darkey Duncan, Short Bear, and Billy Buttons, who wore a black band around his arm. Dora wore a black hat and a black skirt and blouse. The face she turned toward me was a mask of misery.

Darkey Duncan hulked forward on his bench, glowering at me. Short Bear, knifeless, regarded me with his face turned away, his black eyes switched toward me. Billy Buttons sat with his hands clasped together. The bank of pearl buttons on his shirt glittered in a sun ray. He was armed with a cartridge belt and a holstered .44.

I had a sense that there had been some discussion as to whether it would have been preferable if Oz Bird had found his proper target.

"What now?" I said, seating myself beside Dora.

"He's been here," Duncan said. "Miss Dory's seen him. Billy's seen him."

"We watch," Short Bear grunted.

"What does he intend?" I said to Dora.

She tucked her lips in tight, looking down at her hands. She shook her neat head once.

"To carry you off?" I said.

"You must show Tom the letter, Miss Dory," Billy said.

She drew a sheet of paper from her bosom and unfolded it. It was heavy vellum with a black border almost an inch wide. It was signed "Victoria R." and headed "My Dear Mrs. Studely." It was a letter from Queen Victoria, some of it illegible because the spidery handwriting ran off into the black border on both sides of the page:

> *I must express personally my deep and heartfelt sympathy with you under the shocking circum- stances of this terrible calamity. No one can better appreciate than I can, who am myself utterly brokenhearted by the loss of my own beloved husband, who was the light of my life, my stay, my all, what your sufferings must be; and I earnestly pray that you may be supported by Him to Whom alone the sorely stricken can look for comfort, in this hour of heavy affliction.*

"She refers to you as Mrs. Studely," I said.

"I had to be presented to her in that way, or she would not have received me."

"What a wonderful letter," I said.

She refolded it carefully and replaced it inside her bodice.

"It is a valuable letter, Mr. Boxcroft says."

A cowhand appeared in the doorway. "That Sergeant Maule's all ready out there, Miss Dora!"

She rose, straightened her shoulders, and took up her little silver-chased rifle from the bench beside her. Without another glance at me, as though she had turned in upon herself in readiness for this contest of skills, or perhaps confronting the fact of Bird circling closer, she accompanied the cowhand outside, carrying the rifle. I was left with her three guardians.

"Bird thinks she will go off with him," I said. "She thinks he has Argentina in mind."

Jutting his shark jaw, Short Bear tossed a hand in the air, staring at it with a cross-eyed intensity that made me stare at it, too, as though it held a knife. *"Dead man!"* he said.

Duncan sat looking down at his dark fist.

I went out with Billy Buttons to watch the match.

It was not much of a contest; Dora and Sergeant Maule stood at two stands, shooting at clay pigeons tossed up by a man with a machine of some kind, concealed behind a hillock of dirt. Sergeant Maule was a skinny soldier in khaki, with chevrons on his sleeve, gleaming leather puttees, and a conical hat. His nervousness was obvious. At the one-hundred mark he was five behind.

There were perhaps fifty people watching from the stands. The contest was boring inside a heavy shell of anxiety.

I went to Colonel Studely's tent looking for Mr. Boxcroft. He was there, rising from a chair to offer me his hand.

"That is a fine letter from Queen Victoria," I said.

"Worth its weight," Boxcroft said. "Common-law marriage depends upon intent, the woman being treated and spoken of as wife. You could hardly have a more effective witness than the Queen of England."

"So the Show is Miss Pratt's. I wonder if she cares."

"I understand it was you Oz Bird thought he was shooting, Redmond."

I nodded. The slow statement and response of the rifle contest in the Fairgrounds sounded very close.

"You are in danger, then," Boxcroft said. "I wonder if you would join me in a glass of Old Crow, while our heroine demolishes the pretenses of that skinny sergeant."

He indicated a chair, and I seated myself. The popping of the two rifles punctuated the silence as Boxcroft produced a bottle and poured the two glasses.

He told stories of the Show's career, mainly cheerful ones. I was impressed by his loquacity. He did not, however, seem to wish to discourse on Dora's establishment as a common-law wife.

In one of the pauses in the shooting, he said, "I do wish that little lady the best of luck in all her life."

When I left the big tent to go back to see how the contest was progressing, it was over. No one was left in the stands, and the center of the Fairgrounds was deserted. A cluster of performers hovered around the Concord coach, with its team of mules slapping tails and craning necks. One of the men ran toward me, slow in his boots and chaps. It was Billy Buttons, with his mouth wrenched open panting.

"Tom, Oz's in there with her! Him and a big lout of a fellow with him!" He pointed toward the barn, with its corrugated tin roof gleaming in the sun. I started toward it at a pace of half haste, half reluctance. All at once I was breathing hard.

In the sudden shadow of the barn I heard a harsh, resonant voice, but I could see no one. I swung eight feet up the ladder to the loft and hurried along the aisle between the bales. Where the platform ended I could see down to the lower floor. Dora stood among the bales in a black jacket spotted with hay dust, hatless, her rifle slanted forward, facing the back of the barn.

I started to call to her, but the intensity of her posture stopped me. A man stepped out of the shadows opposite me, his rifle pointed, a big hat shading his face. Jukes. I could smell him as he poked the rifle toward me. I raised my hands. Below us Dora had seen nothing of this, facing whatever she was facing.

Oz Bird's voice came again. "Go ahead and shoot me, little honey. Come on, shoot your husbin, you have did everything else to him. Just you shoot him now!"

Dora did not move, but held her rifle angled before her.

"Come on, honey pussy," Bird's resonant voice came again. "Shoot me in the balls while you're at it, that taught you to shoot like a angel."

Dora's rifle barrel twitched.

Bird laughed.

"You are my wedded wife, little honey. That swore some big swears you would honor and obey."

"I am not married to you!"

"Give you some good lovin', honey pot."

"You are a monster," Dora whispered.

With my hands raised, inching one foot toward the edge of the hayloft platform, then the other, I could see Bird standing back in the shadows, facing Dora, not apparently armed.

"Shoot the monster, little honey!" he called.

"I will not shoot a human being!"

"Shot that sandlapper farmer down at Hungry Valley, din't you?"

I could see Jukes's features in the shadow of his hat's brim. He had the face of a clever simpleton. The muzzle of his rifle was a round spot of pitchier darkness directed at me.

Dora held her rifle in the same ready position. I did not think she would shoot Oz Bird.

Bird took a step forward. The barrel of Dora's rifle twitched up. Jukes's rifle tilted toward her at the motion. Bird laughed a forced laugh. He stood with his arms folded on his chest.

I stifled a sneeze from the dust in the air. The muzzle of Jukes's rifle jabbed toward me. Bird slid a leg forward. Now a ray of gray light from a split in the barn wall sliced across him. His whiskered, dark face was cemented in a grin.

"Don't come any further," Dora whispered. Her rifle tipped again. Jukes's tipped with it.

"Shoot me, then, little honey," Bird said, and came on.

He halted twenty feet from her.

"Don't come any closer," Dora whispered.

If I jumped Jukes when his rifle tipped toward her—

"No further!"

Oz Bird stretched his arms toward her.

"Help me!" she cried.

In a sudden stir of motion, someone burst from behind the bales beside her. Bird made a kind of squawk, his hands grasping at a black peg that had appeared on his throat. Another appeared on his chest. He staggered back and fell.

Jukes's rifle exploded as he leaned toward the edge of the platform. Below me, Short Bear staggered like Bird, sprawling. Dora's rifle swung up and cracked. Jukes's rifle leaped from his hands. I jumped him.

I caught a glimpse of Dora's white face as Jukes and I slid, grasping at each other, from the hayloft and slammed down beside her.

His hands were stronger than mine. He was on top of me, his big red face snarling into mine, his hands on my throat. He was too much for me. I couldn't breathe!

Dora cried, *"Darkey!"*

Jukes's hands were torn from my throat. Flat on the floor, I saw him hauled up, his head clasped between Darkey Duncan's big hands. Darkey swung his body like a sack against one of the posts, and flung him down where Short Bear lay.

As I struggled to my feet I saw Duncan stride toward Bird and kick him.

Dora cast her rifle aside and showed me her open hands. Her eyes were despairing. She ran to me.

There was then an interminable business of police sent for, and a doctor sent for, and Short Bear borne off in an ambulance, and the bodies of Oz Bird and his man Jukes taken off in a wagon to the morgue, and more police coming, and Chief O'Brien coming last of all. Darkey Duncan and Billy Buttons stood by throughout, and a dozen other performers from the Show came into the barn to wish Dora well. Dora remained seated on a hay bale with her fingers locked together, answering the questions that had to be answered and once in a while glancing my way with an expression of exhaustion.

In the end I was able to bear her off in a hack to the Cyrus Hotel. I accompanied her up the stairs, her hand heavy on my arm. In her room she threw herself down on the bed and began to weep in great heaving sobs. I sat beside her bed, leaning over her.

"Poor Oz!" she whispered to me. And then, "Poor Robbie!" And a little later, "Poor Eva!" And still later, "I don't even know that other man's name!"

"Jukes."

I stroked her hand.

"Poor Jukes!" she said. Her eyes were closed. The sun slanted in the window and across the bed, and touched with blue the tears on her cheeks.

"It's over, Dora," I said, although I knew it was not.

"Tom, would you go to ask Louisa Keith to come to see me? I promised her . . . I promised her . . ."

I departed to do so. Miss Keith would be writing Dora Pratt's history, as Oz Bird had demanded that I write his, which now would be written in memoriam.

CHAPTER TWENTY-TWO

SATIETY, n. The feeling that one has for the plate after he has eaten its contents, madam.

— *The Devil's Dictionary*

THURSDAY, MARCH 31, 1892

Bierce did not seem much surprised to learn of the disposition of Oz Bird and Jukes.

"So," he said, "God protect the right!"

"God and the brotherhood," I said.

Just then Miss Keith turned into his office, smiling at me as I rose, addressing Bierce as he slanted a hand to gesture her to a chair.

"*Rational procreation* is another term for Eugenics, Mr. Bierce," she announced.

"Is that so, Miss Keith?"

"Still another is *stirpiculture,*" she continued, settling in. "Of which I am a product, you see."

"Please explain, Miss Keith," Bierce said.

"Have you heard the name of John Humphrey Noyes?"

"The Oneida Colony!" Bierce said.

"Community, if you please," Miss Keith said. "They—I can no longer say we—called themselves Perfectionists."

162

"Free love, one was given to understand."

"Complex marriage," Miss Keith said. "It is very different. One was married to all."

"Nevertheless—"

"Very different," Miss Keith insisted. "A woman could not be addressed directly in regard to a 'transaction,' but must be approached through a third party. Exclusive bonds between two persons were expressly forbidden. Not so very free, Mr. Bierce, Mr. Redmond."

It occurred to me, shamefully, that out of simple jealousy I did not break into this flow of information to tell Miss Keith that Dora wanted to see her.

"Nor free as to childbearing, as I recall," Bierce said.

"Conception of children was expressly forbidden!"

"And how was that accomplished, Miss Keith?"

"It was accomplished through male continence."

Bierce frowned down his nose at her, whose cheeks had turned pink.

"Transactions were for the gratification of what Father Noyes called 'the amative instinct,'" Miss Keith hurried on. "Procreation must be scientifically planned and approved. Of which, as I said, I am a product."

"Of your gratified mother and father," Bierce said, "was your father known to you?"

"He was not," Miss Keith said. She brushed a hand at her hair. "He may well have been Father Noyes himself."

"That scoundrel!" Bierce said.

"That genius, rather!" Miss Keith said, raising her chin combatively.

"Same thing," Bierce said. "He was brought down by protestant clergymen, I believe. Of the ilk of Henry Ward Beecher, of whom it was said that as many as forty of his mistresses attended his sermons."

"The newspapers as well as the clergy were dedicated to the Perfectionists' downfall!"

"So your mother submitted to Father Noyes or another, for the purpose of you," Bierce said.

"Submitted is not a word she would have used," Miss Keith said. "Nor did we have a relation in which such a subject could have been discussed. Perfectionist progeny were not reared by their parents, but by suitable members trained for that purpose. The idea, you see, was to prevent the idolatrous love of mother and child."

"And somehow you became a perfectly rational human being, albeit a poetess."

Miss Keith smiled gently. "I am afaid I am a Perfectionist apostate. Father Noyes is long dead, and the Oneida Community has gone over to Spiritualism."

"But stirpiculture did not proceed to the logical conclusions of Eugenics," Bierce said. "Where inferior citizens were to be sterilized in order to raise the quality of the race?"

"It did not! It may seem, Mr. Bierce, that I make light of my provenance. I am proud of it! I hold Father Noyes in the highest regard, and I applaud his thought and efforts to perfect his community. I do not think he would have done violence to any he deemed unfit members of the race."

I broke in at last to announce the death of Oswald Bird.

"And what of Miss Pratt?" Miss Keith inquired.

"She is at her hotel. She asks to speak with you."

Miss Keith departed hurriedly.

I informed Bierce of the events at the Fairgrounds, which at least had left Dora Pratt free of her ex-husband, and of the letter from the queen.

I told him that I had never heard the term *stirpiculture* before.

"It refers to the breeding of special stock."

He then proceeded to a meeting with Willie Hearst and Sam Chamberlain, and I to begin writing the gee-whiz story of the deaths of the murderous outlaw Oswald Bird and his accomplice.

When I had turned my story over to Sam Chamberlain for editing, Bierce asked me to go for a stroll in Chinatown with him, which meant he needed a pipe or three of opium to settle his mental processes.

We headed up Dupont Street, into the outlandish architecture of upturned eaves, latticed balconies, and colored columns. Bulletins two feet high inscribed with a maze of graceful black calligraphy and bordered in red adorned the corners of buildings. The small shops displayed curios, embroidery, bronzes, jades, ivory, carved coral, and stacks of green dishes, along with apothecary stocks of Chinese remedies. Most of the men bustling by were dressed in black pajamas and flat-brimmed hats with pigtails, though some wore Western clothing. Street peddlers with pushcarts and portable stands offered Chinese cakes, candies, nuts, and cigars.

Bierce and I made our way through these amid the smells of incense and urine, and down an alley decorated with green and red lanterns. We descended steps to an ironbound door, which opened seemingly by magic. Inside, the sweetish stench of opium hit us in a wave. A tall Chinese man bowed us through a series of rooms, in which men, not all of them Chinese, reclined on wooden bunks. On a wall was a price list for small pipes and large.

Bierce was directed to a cot, and the host helped him off with his jacket. Bierce indicated a straight chair, which the man, bowing, brought over for me.

A young attendant appeared, squatting beside the taboret at

Bierce's right side, kneading a ball of dark gum over a flame until it softened. Then he plunged it into the bowl of a pipe. Bierce inhaled this while a second pipe was prepared.

He said to me, "Tell me everything I know and don't know."

We'd been through this before. I talked, and from time to time Bierce asked a sleepy question.

"The imagination begins to run like a clear stream," he confided in me. "It is an ugly business, Tom. It is not complete."

Oz Bird had been a sideshow, like Ike Guttman.

"It is an ugly business, Tom," Bierce said again. "I think I do not wish to see this through to its conclusion."

FRIDAY, APRIL 1, 1892

In the morning the headlines read

FAMOUS WINGSHOT IN CUSTODY

....

TWO HUSBANDS DEAD IN ONE MONTH

....

COMMON-LAW WIFE OF COL. STUDELY

....

CHAPTER TWENTY-THREE

EDUCATION, n. That which discloses to the wise and disguises from the foolish their lack of understanding.

— The Devil's Dictionary

FRIDAY, APRIL 1, 1892

With Willie Hearst in his office were Sam Chamberlain— dressed to the nines, or maybe tens, with a carnation in his buttonhole and his monocle hanging from its black string—and chief of detectives Dan O'Brien, standing stiffly tall with his beard-framed chin and his disapproving mouth. Willie sat behind his desk with an expression on his face that was smug, with a dash of anxiety.

Bierce halted just inside the door so that I had to edge past him. "Mr. Bierce," Willie said. "Mr. Redmond. We believe the Studely case is now closed."

"It is not!" Bierce said, in a low, harsh voice. "Why have you done this?" he said to Sam, who lounged not at ease in his chair beside Willie's desk.

"It worked, Ambrose!" Sam said, rearranging his long legs in his chair. "We thought this case of murder had gone on long enough. When the fact of Miss Pratt's common-law marriage was revealed, we arranged the headline that would persuade Chief O'Brien here to take her into custody. Whereupon the actual culprit has declared himself."

"Confessed to back-shooting his boss," Chief O'Brien said, nodding.

"He is not the culprit," Bierce said.

"Confessed in front of witness!" O'Brien said.

"Now, see here, Mr. Bierce—" Willie started.

"This newspaper has committed an irreparable wrong," Bierce said. "You will have my resignation this morning, Mr. Hearst!"

"Now, just a minute, Mr. Bierce—" Willie started.

"You put me in charge of this investigation, then you allowed Sam Chamberlain to commit this clownish error!"

Chief O'Brien cleared his throat for attention. He advanced a step toward Bierce. "See here," he said. "I surely don't have any sympathies for Oz Bird. But if that weren't a conspired-on bushwhack, I never heard of one. Mrs. Studely surely set out to trap Oz Bird, with her pals standing by, one of them the knife-throwing champ and the other a nigger man-beater, as we saw with the Butcher Boy last month. Drawn that poor fool along till he got in range of the redskin. If that weren't what happened, I'll be pleased to hear another version!"

"That is not the issue whatsoever, Chief," Bierce said in a disgusted tone. "Moreover, Mr. Redmond here saw the whole business."

O'Brien paced, his hands clasped behind him, while I told him my version of the death of Oz Bird. He halted and fixed me with a gaze that was supposed to paralyze liars.

"Just tell me how that lady was in danger! Bird wasn't even heeled."

"His partner was up in the hayloft with me, with a rifle aimed at Miss Pratt."

"So you say, that has a fondness on Miss Pratt, which is well known about town!"

"That has nothing to do with what I saw."

"I will tell you something else," the chief of detectives said to me. "It is police experience that when there is a murder of a spouse, the surviving spouse is the number-one suspect! And Miss Pratt was Studely's and Bird's both. How do you answer that?"

"So Mrs. Arliff J. Potter is also in custody?" I asked.

"Miss Pratt is no longer in custody," Sam put in, glancing nervously at Bierce.

"That young Buttons fellow has confessed!" Sam said.

"He is not the culprit!" Bierce said. "You have begotten a tragedy, gentlemen, and I wash my hands of it!"

He knocked against me, swinging around to start out.

"Mr. Bierce!" Willie Hearst said, standing, tall and pale, his nose bisecting his long countenance, as straight as a ruler's edge.

Bierce turned back. His face was dark with anger.

"Mr. Bierce, do you align yourself with Pontius Pilate in the matter of hand washing?"

Bierce glared at him.

"Mr. Bierce, you *are* in charge of this matter! I apologize for our interference, but I will demand of you that you reveal the true culprit, if it is not young Buttons!"

Bierce swung around again, and, without another word, stamped out of the office. I grimaced apologetically at the assembled, and followed him.

In his office he flung himself down in his chair and glared at me over the grinning, chalky skull. He picked up a pencil and snapped it between his fingers, flinging the pieces down.

"I had hoped this cup would pass from me!" he said.

"I don't know what you mean."

"Willie is right, and I must see it through, in spite of their damnable interference. Tom, will you return to that odious trio and see that a general meeting is arranged? I must have those three, Miss Pratt and her lawyer—Mr. Boxcroft—and Miss Keith. And Professor Franklyn, if he can be persuaded to assist us. They will arrange a meeting, at which I will preside."

"Billy Buttons?" I asked.

He considered the idea. "Yes, I suppose so."

"Darkey Duncan?"

He shook his head. "Please go now, while I try to regain control of myself. Willie Hearst will have my resignation as soon as this matter is unhappily concluded."

He continued, "The key to this matter is Colonel Studely as a Eugenicist."

I returned to Willie Hearst's office. The three there appeared paralyzed.

Sam would take charge of assembling the group Bierce had demanded.

....

The meeting had been arranged for three o'clock. Bierce delayed another ten minutes before he and I set out for Willie Hearst's office.

Chairs were arranged in a semicircle facing Willie's desk; each was occupied when we entered. Dora wore a bottle-green gown. She had removed the matching cap. Sunlight gleamed through the window onto her sleek head. She glanced at me and then away, as though we hardly knew one another.

Miss Keith sat on one side of her, Boxcroft on the other. Next to him was Billy Buttons, clad in a high collar and a dark suit. He seemed to be suffering from a chill; his jaw trembled. Dora reached across the lawyer to pat the boy's hand. "Miss Dory!" he whispered.

On the other side of the desk were Sam Chamberlain and

Chief O'Brien. Willie stood behind the desk as Bierce and I entered. Professor Franklyn had departed from San Francisco three days earlier, so was not in attendance.

"Gentlemen and ladies, we are here to solve these crimes that have been brought to a head by the demise of Oswald Bird," Willie began. "It is believed that Bird did not shoot Colonel Studely. It is Chief O'Brien's contention that in a spousal crime, the surviving spouse is the primary suspect. With this in mind, he summoned Miss Pratt for questioning. Her fellow performer Billy Buttons then confessed to the crime. Mr. Bierce, will you now proceed?" He seated himself.

"I will ask Miss Pratt for a response," Bierce said.

"Billy could not have done it," Dora said calmly. "I was riding next to him, behind Colonel Studely. I would have known if he had fired his rifle."

"Then why has this young fellow confessed, Miss Pratt?" Sam Chamberlain wanted to know.

"He believed he was protecting me."

"Miss Pratt," Bierce said, "you say you would have known if this young fellow had shot Studely. Consequently, he would also have known if you had fired the shot?"

She looked at Bierce with her clear-eyed gaze. "He would."

"I understand why he would make this gesture," Miss Keith said, leaning forward. Her hands drifted out before her as if she didn't know what to do with them. "Miss Pratt has her protectors, you see. Mr. Buttons is one of these. However, he failed to be on hand for the fatal confrontation with Oswald Bird."

"There is that," Bierce said. "But most likely, Buttons served as Bird's spy as to Miss Pratt's actions. He had always been Bird's penny boy. It seems he was properly guilty about it."

"Miss Dory, I didn't mean—!" Billy cried out. This time she did not look at him.

Bierce said, "Bird made the common male error of assuming that a woman, once enamored of him, would always respond."

Miss Keith nodded to him.

Bierce said, "The assumption has been that the murderer of Colonel Studely thought that Bird would be blamed for the act. It is a matter of motive."

"It is a matter of the ownership of the colonel's Wild West Show!" Boxcroft said. He leaned back with his arms folded on his chest. "Miss Pratt is the owner. Her status as the common-law wife of Colonel Studely cannot now be contested!"

"Colonel Studely was an adherent of the Eugenics philosophy," Bierce said.

Miss Keith laid her hands to her cheeks, watching Dora, who gazed steadily at Bierce. Boxcroft patted Dora's hand.

"There was a child," Bierce continued. "The child, Evalina, was defective. Colonel Studely believed that defective children should be done away with for the health of the race. Is that not so, Miss Pratt?"

"Yes, it is true!" Dora said, her chin up.

"The fact that Studely's own child was defective was an especial insult to him. He called her an idiot, a moron, a booby. He tried to hire an assassin to dispose of his shame. The assassin, however, had the conscience not to murder a helpless child. What did Studely do then, Miss Pratt?"

"He went to St. Louis," Dora said. "We had a nurse, Miss Pugh. Colonel Studely offered to give the child her bath, and made a clamor that Evalina had drowned. He had done it himself! He told me he had done it. He wept. Pretended to weep. He begged my forgiveness."

"This was at the time of the dispute over Buttons's dog?"

"Yes."

"And you did not forgive him."

"I did not, Mr. Bierce.

"So you shot your husband, Miss Pratt?" Sam said. "Just as the chief surmised!"

"No, I did not," Dora said.

There was silence. Dora continued to gaze at Bierce.

"There is a strangeness when you shoot at targets, Mr. Bierce," she continued, "as I once tried to explain to you. You, the *you* of you, does not think, 'Shoot!' Your eye and hand do that. My hand shot Colonel Studely. I did not think, 'Shoot him!' I had my rifle in my right hand, but on my saddle horn was a cartridge belt with a Peacemaker in the holster. My hand drew the Peacemaker from the holster and fired it. The Peacemaker longed for release, you see. Of course, Billy was aware of it. Rique may have been, also."

"Please don't!" Billy groaned.

"I am grateful, Billy," she said. "You were very brave. But you must know I could not accept your sacrifice."

I thought her beautiful, calm, and courageous.

Still she avoided my eyes. "I have sworn I would never direct a gun at a human being, but it has happened twice. Because there is a malevolence in guns. Because there is a lust in them to point at someone, foe or friend, and fire. To bully, to hurt, to maim, to kill. I warn you against guns, gentlemen. One will never dominate my hand again!"

"There you have it, then!" O'Brien said, standing. He dusted his hands together as though certain he had been in the right all along. I felt as though the bottom had dropped out of me. Willie Hearst glanced apprehensively at Bierce.

"I wish there could have been another solution, Miss Pratt," Bierce said.

"Just a minute!" I said, just as Boxcroft called out, "Wait!"

Dora rose to her feet. Now her eyes fixed calmly on mine.

"You worried because I was sad, Tom. This is why I have been sad. I am very glad to get it off my shoulders. I will be sad no more!"

"That devil murdered your defenseless child!" Boxcroft spluttered.

"An obsession with Eugenics is a terrible thing, gentlemen!" Miss Keith said in her uncontentious voice. "Colonel Studely could not bear anything defective, as I have learned from Miss Pratt. He could especially not bear that such a defective being could be a failure of his own loins. The Eugenicists demand inhuman remedies! Mr. Duncan has been the victim of this terrible attitude from Colonel Studely, because of his race. Poor people have been the victims of it. As though one pauper begets a battalion of them!"

"Never mind it, Miss Keith," Dora said, stepping toward O'Brien. Miss Keith laid her hands to her cheeks again, watching Dora as though she were a heroine in tragic action.

And so, accompanied by the chief of detectives, my beloved turned toward the door without another glance at me. When Boxcroft rose to accompany her, she said, "It's all right, Boxy."

"Just a minute!" Sam said. "But who killed Potter?"

"Bird," Bierce said. "Who did not deny it, as he did the murder of Colonel Studely."

He took a sheet of paper from his pocket and stepped forward to drop his resignation on Willie Hearst's desk. The others began to rise and mill.

I caught up with Dora and Chief O'Brien in the hallway, as the chief buttoned himself into a blue overcoat. Dora glanced at me, thin-lipped; then she smiled at me.

"That is for you!" she whispered.

We turned outside into a windy day on Montgomery Street.

A little man in a black slouch hat and a black overcoat stood just outside the door. Black eyes blazed at Dora from a pure white face. The man produced a revolver as big as his head and aimed it at her.

"Miz Oswald Bird, meet your husbin in hell!"

It was Ike Guttman, Gizzard. I stepped in front of Dora.

"What is this?" O'Brien yelled.

"Bitch kilt my boy! Get outen the way there, you, or I'll gut the two of you!"

Just then Bierce appeared in the doorway, his revolver drawn, his finger pointed along the barrel. With a curse, Guttman swung his weapon toward Bierce.

There was a revolver blast like a slap in the face.

Guttman seemed to shrink. His revolver remained leveled at Bierce as his knees gave way. He went down as though deflating. He sprawled on the sidewalk at Chief O'Brien's feet, his hat rolling free from a head as bald as a baseball.

O'Brien said in a shaky voice, "That was a considerable help, Mr. Bierce!"

Her mouth gaping in anguish, Dora cried hoarsely, "Why didn't you let him? Do you think I want to be *hanged?*"

Bierce stepped toward her. He said sternly, "Miss Pratt, you will not be hanged! You may spend a month or two in prison, but you will be pardoned, I promise you! And you will spend the rest of your life as you desire!"

Dora sobbed in my arms.

Bierce said calmly, "Would it be a benefit if you took these honors on yourself, Chief O'Brien?"

"It would!" O'Brien said.

Bierce's revolver disappeared, and O'Brien's produced itself. O'Brien was to acclaimed the hero of this encounter.

I gazed down at Oz Bird's father, whom Bird had wished to celebrate in his history of a family of shootists.

CHAPTER TWENTY-FOUR

MOSAIC, n. *A kind of inlaid work. From Moses, who when little was inlaid in a basket among the bulrushes.*
— *The Devils' Dictionary*

MONDAY, APRIL 4, 1892

A few days later I encountered Willie Hearst in the second-floor hallway of the *Examiner* building.

"Ah, Mr. Redmond! You are to be congratulated on the fine piece you wrote on the Colonel Studely affair! Very well done, Mr. Redmond!"

Gee whiz! "Thank you, Mr. Hearst!"

"Ah, Mr. Redmond! Any word from Mr. Bierce?"

"Not a word," I said.

No doubt Bierce had holed up in one of his usual havens in an asthma-free hamlet away from San Francisco: Crane's Hotel in Sunol, the Putnam House in Auburn, Angwin's on Howell Mountain, El Monte in Los Gatos, or Wright's in the Santa Cruz mountains.

Willie sighed and said, "I hate to travel to some godforsaken mountain to persuade him to come back to the *Examiner*.

Mr. Chamberlain has volunteered for the task, but I'm afraid, this time, considering the degree of the offense, I will have to humble myself. Good day, Mr. Redmond," said the proprietor and publisher of the San Francisco *Examiner,* and passed on down the hall, politely greeting reporters and secretaries as he progressed.

....

Bierce's office had been locked, but apparently the cleaning person had left the door ajar, so I went inside to pat the cranium of the desk skull.

A burly young man in a black frock coat came in behind me. He had a pugnacious look.

"I'm looking for Mr. Bierce!"

"Not here. Resigned from the paper and gone."

"I went by his place on Broadway. Not there, either."

"He's in the mountains somewhere. For his asthma."

"I'd like to give him some asthma!" he said, raising a thick fist. "Playing games with my wife!"

"You'd be Mr. Merkle?"

"I'd be Mr. Anderson, husband to Miss Merkle. Who're you?"

I informed him.

"Friend of Bierce's, are you? I want to know where he is at!" He showed me the fist. "She's been there at number fourteen twenty-eight Broadway with him!"

"I assure you that I do not know where he is."

"Who'd know, then?"

"He has communicated with no one at this newspaper."

Mr. Anderson left, muttering.

I was sitting behind Bierce's desk, which was cleared off except for the skull, when Miss Keith looked into the office.

"I thought you might be Ambrose, Tom!"

I went through the same conversation with her regarding Bierce's wherabouts as I had with the angry Mr. Anderson, husband of the charming Miss Merkle.

Miss Keith seated herself facing me. She had the eyes of an angel, but I found myself wishing she had a more proficient hairdresser.

"Have you seen Miss Pratt?" she asked.

"Every day." I had been courting Dora in prison, trying to melt the frozen sea of her.

"Is she in good spirits?"

"It is a curious thing, but she no longer seems so sad. She will be well defended by Bosworth Curtis, you know. "

"And the trial will be next month?"

"On the first Monday."

"Do you suppose Ambrose will return to the *Examiner?*"

"There is a kind of game to be played. Willie Hearst will coax him back with apologies and promises. This has happened several times before. Of course, on some occasion he may choose *not* to return to San Francisco."

"You are his good friend."

I said carefully, "Let's say I am his associate."

"I had supposed that Ambrose and I were friends."

"He has spoken very highly of you," I said, my fingers crossed. Though it was clear enough that Bierce respected her.

She colored, the pink sweeping up her cheeks from her throat, where she laid a hand. "I had thought there might be a romantic association."

I did not say that that would have been more possible if she had not given Bierce her poetry to read and appreciate—or deprecate.

"He suggested an irregular relation that was a shock to me."

"I'm sorry to be of so little help," I said, praying that this revelation would go no further.

And, as if she understood my thought, she smiled and rose, and, still flushed, departed with her quick step.

EPILOGUE

REVIEW, v.t.

To set your wisdom (holding not a doubt of it,
  Although in truth there's neither bone or skin to it)
At work upon a book, and so read out of it
  The qualities that you have first read into it.
    — The Devil's Dictionary

Dora was sentenced to seven years in San Quentin, but in 1893, badgered by Bierce in "Prattle," Governor Nash pardoned her. I took a month's leave from the *Examiner* and she and I entrained for the East to spend some time at Niagara Falls, which she had always wanted to see. There our future was discussed. She had had bad experiences with the two men she had married, if the second one had in fact been a marriage, and didn't wish to marry again. She had given birth to a feebleminded child, and wished to birth no more children.

....

Dora spent hours on one of the slatted benches on Goat Island, hatted, coated, and muffed against the wind-borne spume, gazing out at the American Falls. It became clear to me that she would never be the wife and mother I had hoped for.

She had corresponded with Miss Keith throughout her

prison term, and on our way back West from Niagara Falls, wanted to stop off in Chicago to see her, our, friend, who was now assisting Jane Addams at Hull-House.

Dora Pratt decided to remain in Chicago, where she and Miss Keith became lieutenants to the saintly Miss Addams, cited and praised in her biographies. As far as I know, she kept her vow and never picked up a rifle again.

....

Ted the parrot had been taken to live in New York City with Mr. Boxcroft, who disposed of the Show's assets to pay for Dora Pratt's legal counsel.

....

Short Bear recovered from his wound and, as Colonel Studely's Combination had de-combined because of the matters detailed herein, returned to Oklahoma. He was murdered in a quarrel with Indian agents on the Ponca Reservation in 1896. Darkey Duncan engaged in a second fight with his opponent Iggy Carlinsky. He was knocked out in the twenty-second round. There was no rubber contest. I lost track of him thereafter. Billy Buttons joined Pawnee Bill's Wild West Show, where he performed as a trick rider for years.

....

Henry Borland, who had murdered his wife, dressed her body in his clothes, and presided over his own funeral while assuming her identity, was sentenced and hanged. He commented that his wife was a woman who could not keep her yap shut, but he claimed that his motive was that "they" were after him and by pretending to be dead "they" would let him be.

....

Mrs. Potter, also, maintained that someone from the vigilante past had murdered her husband, although it was Bierce's convinction that Bird was the sniper who had shot Potter.

....

It was never entirely clear whether Ike Guttman was Oz Bird's father or stepfather, although one elderly neighbor suggested that he might have been both, for the mother was a wild one.

....

My own mother was discouraged because another year had passed and I had neither married nor produced a grandchild for her.

....

After a month of boredom at the hotel in Auburn, Bierce allowed himself to be persuaded to come back to the *Examiner*.